A Powerful Season

Kathryn Dodson

Renegade Reads

Contents

Chapter 1

Lacey had waited ten years for this letter. It showed up in a sealed envelope instead of an email attachment, adding to its importance. She pulled the stainless steel letter opener from her desk drawer. It had sat there, barely used, for the last fifteen years, as pixels replaced paper and she'd risen high enough in the organization to acquire an administrative assistant.

She inhaled a wish. Six months, six months would be enough. Then she exhaled the rancor of a potential lawsuit should the number be too low. The envelope's seam parted with a satisfying *skritch*. She pulled out its contents and unfolded the first page.

TWELVE MONTHS! Exactly one month to the day since she'd turned sixty, and they'd offered her the deal of a lifetime. She'd persevered year after year, towing the line the way they'd told her to since business school. Decades of long hours at work, guilt over time spent away from family, and so little time left over for herself. She'd followed the path, climbed the ladder, done everything the right way according to some plan she didn't create. And now, she could finally begin the rest of her life.

She looked around, surprised she couldn't see the monumental shift in the universe that should have occurred. The office walls remained greige instead of the thumping fuchsia her heart desired. The wooden desk stayed solid instead of transforming into molten metal that refashioned itself as a gleaming chariot to whisk her away.

She'd forgotten to breathe. The dried wood pulp and ink now trembled in her unsteady hands. She set the paper down, thoroughly read each page, then pulled an ancient Mont Blanc pen from her desk drawer. The rarely used graduation gift from her parents remained pristine thirty-eight years after its purchase. Other than a phase in the nineties, she'd considered it too ostentatious for the office. She tested it on a piece of paper. Surprisingly, the pen still wrote as smoothly as freedom on a late summer day.

Lacey signed the employment buy-out contract granting her liberty and a generous twelve months of salary and hand-delivered it straight to human resources. She thought she'd escaped after leaving it on the receptionist's desk, but then a familiar voice rang across the office.

"Lacey, come sit for a minute." Julie waved her into the roomy vice president's office. "So, I take it you took the offer?"

"Hell, yes. I can't believe the effective date is in thirty days. I've got far more vacation than that built up." And they'd pay for every vacation day she didn't use.

"I'm sure Justin will want to talk to you about that. Losing you will be a big transition. He's already mentioned bringing you back as a consultant."

"He's the one who said the department needed to head in a new direction." Lacey attempted to straighten her face, certain it held the sneer that comment provoked.

"You challenged him at every turn."

"He knows nothing about our industry and wanted to dismantle the one department in this company that helps all the others attain their goals. His changes would have inevitably damaged the business, and the higher ups would blame me, not the new wonder boy. I was trying to save my ass and the company's bottom line."

"Well, your ass is now duly saved." A genuine smile lit Julie's face. "And you got a hell of a deal out of it—one year's severance. Plus, you can set your rate as a consultant. I know Justin wants your expertise, just not in his chain of command."

"Justin can suck my dick." Lacey slapped her hand across her mouth, shocked that the comment had slipped out. She'd heard the line in a movie and loved the moxie of the teenage character. It sounded ridiculous coming out of her sixty-year-old mouth, but the excitement of breaking a rule zinged through her, nonetheless.

Julie looked at her in shock, then started giggling. "Well, he can't force you to consult," she said once her laughter stopped.

Exhilaration flooded Lacey. After all these years, she drove the bus. She'd never have to hold back her tongue or work a single day she didn't want to. This very minute, she could walk out, claim unused vacation days, and never return. She sure as hell wouldn't come back as a consultant. She certainly wouldn't stay for thirty days so the child prodigy could set her up to take the fall for his disastrous decisions.

"He's not so bad," Julie said. "Just inexperienced."

Lacey agreed with Julie's assessment, but it hadn't been her choice to put a twenty-nine-year-old in charge of someone in their sixties. No, that had been Bob's decision.

Bob, one of the last boomers still hanging around the office, had stumbled into the title of Chief Information Officer despite hardly being able to use his iPhone, not to mention the company's array of hardware and software. Somehow, despite his incompetence, he'd been shoved further and further up the corporate ladder, usually when he became so annoying entire divisions threatened to quit. But he'd gone to college with the CEO, which apparently meant lifetime job security.

"Perhaps you're right, and Justin is merely inexperienced. Bob, however, is incompetent. Either way, I plan on using two weeks of vacation over the next month." The satisfaction of the cat eating the canary ran through her, the yellow feathers tasting of lemon candy.

"You should speak to Justin about that. I'm not sure that works with his plans."

A tangerine and black bird flitted in a tree outside Julie's window, jumping from branch to branch and shaking the dark green leaves. A world bright with color waited for her. Maybe she'd take the afternoon off and experience warm sunshine on her face instead of returning to her greige cage.

She turned to Julie, a friend, but one who counseled others in the company. "I am sixty years old, and I have earned my vacation. You might want to remind the twenty-nine-year-old about age discrimination."

"What's gotten into you? You've never been quite so ornery before." Julie's surprise at her reaction had turned to concern.

"Don't you ever want to get out of here? You're almost my age. How long are you going to stay?"

"As long as they keep paying me. I've got kids in college, and I'm the major breadwinner." Julie's face turned grim.

As Lacey stared back at her friend, lifelong responsibilities unshackled themselves from her shoulders. Her kids had done well. Maddie had earned a spot on the partner track at an environmental law firm in San Francisco. Zach, well, he'd decided to follow the early career of his favorite president and become a community organizer, although he'd recently begun working in Oakland's housing and community development department. His passion for his work exceeded anything she'd ever felt, although she worried about his low salary.

The world had changed one hundred and eighty degrees since her graduation. She'd loved literature so much she'd majored in it, but she'd also minored in business. At her first full-time job, they'd paid for higher education, so she'd earned an MBA at night school. She'd been told if she worked hard and saved her money, she'd have a good life and be able to afford retirement. So, she had. And she would.

The bird that had caught her attention flew away. Lacey jerked to a stand. "I've got to go. Please let my superiors know I've accepted their agreement."

Julie's eyebrows raised. "You can't just leave. You have to tell your staff. After all, you don't want them finding this out from Justin, do you?"

Shit. She'd been so absorbed in her own feelings she'd forgotten about everyone else. She glanced down at her phone, ten a.m. "Listen. This is a big change, and I need a little time to process it. Can you hold off on sharing the news until this afternoon? I'll schedule a staff meeting for one o'clock and tell everyone then."

She needed time to think. Her dream had come true, but the next steps eluded her. What would she do this afternoon, tomorrow, three months from now?

As soon as Julie agreed, Lacey stopped by her office and grabbed her purse. On the way out the door, she asked her assistant to schedule the staff meeting. After that, who knew?

Lacey drove toward the ocean. She'd lived in Southern California half her life, and whenever she had a problem, life event, or some extra time on her hands, the water called to her.

Today, she didn't take the shortest path. For once, time had less meaning in her overscheduled days. Instead of racing her to some unknown destination, time sprawled before her, vast and unused, waiting. Its siren song beckoned yet warned her of dangers ahead. Could she survive a life not stuffed with meetings, tasks, and chores? It was damn sure time to find out.

She passed a retirement community of that special California brand. Low slung condos built in the fifties or sixties, about the time of her birth, stretched along a hilltop with an ocean view. It reminded her of the development where she'd once visited her friend Deb's mother. In fact, it might be that very complex. The condos weren't exactly shabby, but they looked dated. Of course, she probably couldn't buy one for less than a million bucks, at least not one with an ocean view.

She drove into Carlsbad's quaint center, currently stuffed with tourists on a warm August day. At her favorite hidden parking lot, she waited for an empty space, then walked down to the sea-wall and followed a concrete pedestrian path along the beach. She leaned on the wall, her face toward the ocean. A light breeze caressed her. Perhaps it had arrived from Hawaii, Japan, or some other faraway place she longed to visit. And now she could. The possibilities seemed as vast as the ocean.

For all her dreams about retirement, she'd never planned what she'd actually do when the day arrived. She'd assumed things would fall into place—exotic destinations to visit and friends to hang out with would reveal themselves. Now she faced a gulf between career woman and happily retired with no straight path from here to there. A trace of worry ran up her spine, her career as a project planner coming home to roost. She'd planned everything but the last third of her life.

But she didn't have to worry about that yet. Today, she wanted to sprint through the sand like a teenager, strip down to bra and undies, and throw herself in the water. She might if she didn't have a meeting to attend. She'd remain presentable for two more weeks then go feral. She wouldn't shower for days, would eat popcorn in her bathrobe and plan some grand adventure. That was the social contract, right? She'd held up her end of the bargain, worked hard, gotten ahead—or at least hadn't fallen behind. Now it was her turn to kick back and let others toil.

Like her kids. She'd go see them first, maybe over a long weekend. They worked so hard, trying to save the world from climate change and social ills. She'd once hoped by the time they had jobs, work life would have changed, no longer requiring the extraordinary hours she'd put in while proving herself.

A different fire burned in them. They didn't work to climb a ladder, but because the world verged on falling apart. Keeping it together had descended onto their shoulders.

Lacey wasn't quite sure how this had happened. Always staunchly pro-environment, pro-feminism, pro-abortion, and anti-discrimination, the world devolved despite her beliefs. How could debates continue on these issues after so long? And how could nothing have helped? She'd recycled, worn a pink pussy hat, voted, given money to the right candidates. Her whole life, she'd done her best.

And yet, these battles had fallen to her children. She shook her head, letting the breeze ruffle her pixie cut. Right now, she needed to focus on this transition. She could let her hair grow long and soft if she didn't have to take on the big boys in the boardroom. She could switch stilettos for something more comfortable. Everything would change with this hard-won golden retirement.

Lacey took one more deep breath of salty air, imagining the scent of jasmine instead of rotting seaweed and suntan oil. Then she returned to the office with the glee of a countdown thumping alongside her heart.

Chapter 2

Back at the office, Lacey held her staff meeting, then escaped earlier than usual. She couldn't bear another conversation about her leaving. Once she'd told her employees, the word had spread like a California wildfire, and she'd dealt with a string of emails, countless phone calls, and a line at her door.

"What are you going to do now?"

"How can you leave?"

"Are you going to be okay?"

Nothing. Easily. Hell yes. Instead of those four simple words, she'd spent minutes, over and over, explaining her future when she had no idea what it would entail.

She'd wanted peace, but as she entered her empty, two-story home, she had the urge to spin around and leave. It represented the past. She'd raised her kids here, in a good suburban neighborhood uphill from an excellent elementary school. She and her then husband bought the place for what they considered a staggering price for a couple from Texas. A medical instrument company had offered her double her salary to do the same project management work she'd done in Dallas, and she and Sean jumped at the opportunity. He easily found a commercial real estate job in Carlsbad, and they bought the Spanish-style home with four bedrooms, three baths, and a view of Carlsbad, California's rolling hills.

Of course, three years later, he defected back to Texas and soon took up with a secretary at work ten years younger and at least three bra cups larger than Lacey. He now had a second family there, although he'd divorced Miss DDD some time ago. For years she'd tried to hate him for the defection, but he'd been more than fair in the divorce—his price to get out quickly. He had turned out to be a good, if mostly absent, dad. He took the kids for six weeks each summer and flew into town for big events.

When he first decided to leave, he'd asked the family to return to Texas with him, but Lacey and the kids had stayed. The kids begged not to leave their friends, and even Sean admitted Carlsbad offered a beautiful beach, phenomenal schools, and a vast array of athletic, STEM, and creative camps and after school programs for the kids. That, plus her excellent job and the always perfect weather, meant she'd never return to Texas.

Lacey had always followed the rules, until it was time to choose between her career and her husband. She could have kept him, probably, if she'd moved back home, accepted a lower salary, and reintegrated herself into the good-old-boy network. But at the time, the opportunities here had seemed limitless. So she'd broken up a marriage with a man who chose professional comfort—he'd complained about insufficient opportunities to grow his career—over his family.

But that had been so long ago. Now she stood in an empty house. With the kids gone, this home with all its bedrooms and lovely redone kitchen dwarfed her. She didn't need a yard, eight smoke detectors, and three bathrooms to clean. She didn't need to putter around in a home that longed for an army of tiny feet to stampede up and down the stairs and spill jam on the counters. She didn't belong here anymore.

And with her future stretched before her, she didn't want to live solo in a house built for a family. She wished she had a cottage or a condo somewhere, maybe the fifty-five plus community she'd passed on her way to the beach. It had seemed a little ramshackle, but it looked comfortable and right sized. Without a yard and so much less to maintain, she could lock the front door and go wherever her dreams took her.

Surely, she'd find her way if she lived in the right place. She'd received the buy-out of her dreams, but other things needed to change to take full advantage of this next phase of her life, starting with a home fit for a retiree.

Maybe Deb could give her some insight on places like that. After all, her mother had lived in one for years. Lacey slid her phone out of her purse and found Deb in her contacts.

Two hours later, Lacey and Deb perched on barstools at an Italian restaurant where they met for a glass of wine every few weeks. They'd worked together at MedTech when Lacey started and had become fast friends.

"So, you're finally retiring. I'm so jealous." Deb's silky brunette bob swung at her shoulders as she sipped her wine. "Honestly, with the kids still in college and mom needing to go into a nursing home, I don't think I'll ever stop working."

"I didn't know you were thinking about moving your mom to a nursing home. Part of the reason I wanted to talk to you was to find out more about where she lives. I have got to downsize."

"I've been telling you that for years. I don't know why you kept your big home after the kids left."

Lacey took a sip of wine while she considered Deb's words. "I think I was just always too busy to think about moving. That, and it was convenient to work. In Southern California, a short commute is the new mother lode."

"So true. I'm commuting forty-five minutes each way and, it's hell."

"I think I drove past your mom's development earlier today. What's it like to be in a place like that?"

"Well, for starters, you're far too young."

"Deb, I'm sixty and getting older every day. The place is for fifty-five plus."

"Yeah, but my mom's eighty, and she's not nearly the oldest person there. Still, there are some upsides. It's a pretty close-knit community, and she's made some amazing friends through the years. Some of them are trying to help me out with her situation."

"Help you out? How?" It had been far too long since she'd hung out with Deb, who'd begged off their last few wine dates. Lacey wished she'd known about her mother's troubles.

Deb took a gulp of wine, and when she turned back, tears filled her eyes. "She's got dementia. It's not terrible yet, but it's getting worse quickly. She can't live on her own anymore."

"I'm so sorry to hear that." Lacey shook her head, tears coming to her own eyes. Deb had helped her through the period when her dad had gotten dementia years earlier. It had been a particularly horrible way for such a smart man to go.

"Yeah. Me too." A tear slid down Deb's cheek. "And on top of all that, we've got a chicken and egg thing going on with how to get her into a facility and sell the condo so we can afford everything. It really sucks."

"Tell me what's going on. Please. You took in my kids when I flew back to Dallas to take care of my dad and then my mom. Is there any way I can help?" Lacey laid her hand atop Deb's, her heart breaking right along with her friend's.

Deb ran her fingers under her eyes, sweeping away a few mascara streaks. "I wish it were as easy as taking on a couple extra kids for a week. Unfortunately, last year, when Mom redid her condo, the designer took advantage of her. I didn't know she'd gotten so bad. Honestly, I see her at least every other week. She'd become a little forgetful, but you know Mom. She's always been so independent, so I thought things were fine. Then she let it slip how much she'd paid for the job." A sob escaped Deb, and she drained the last of her Chianti.

Lacey signaled the bartender for two more glasses. Fortunately, they were the only two people in the bar, and the restaurant crowd had yet to trickle in. In fact, the lack of patrons was their favorite thing about this place, but Lacey doubted it could survive much longer on a few glasses of wine.

"I'm sorry I'm such a downer tonight," Deb said. "It's just so frustrating. It turns out she spent sixty-eight thousand dollars just to get the bathroom redone. More for the floors and kitchen. It blew through her savings."

"That's terrible." Lacey continued to pat Deb's hand. She ached for her friend as she remembered her own father's decline.

"Shortly after that, I took her to see a neurologist. Her form of dementia is fast acting, which is why we need to go ahead and consider long-term care."

"I'm so sorry. What will you do?"

"She still has Dad's pension and social security, but to get her into my favorite facility, she'll need a $100,000 deposit."

"Wow. That's steep." Her father's facility hadn't had that type of upfront expense. Not that she'd been proud to put him there. She'd carried the guilt of that decision for years. She would figure her own life out and have a plan in place so she didn't leave her children to make such terrible decisions.

"Yeah. She has to purchase an apartment, which she'll live in for the time being. She doesn't need twenty-four-hour care yet, but where she is now is just a condo. I'd prefer she live in a place with a monitored door where they'll see her coming and going. When she can no longer live on her own, they have an assisted care facility on site. The staff is wonderful, and it's close enough for us to visit as often as we want. I'm determined to find a way to make it happen.

The two-hundred-thousand-dollar check Lacey would receive soon flitted through her mind. She thought about her big, lonely home. "So, what's your next step?"

"We need to get her place on the market. Luckily, the remodel looks fantastic. I'm having a realtor go by on Saturday. Given the comps in the community, she thinks it will sell for $525,000."

"That's nothing for being so close to the ocean."

"Well, it was built in the sixties and the exterior looks like it. Plus, it's the smallest size unit and doesn't have an ocean view. There's also a hefty HOA fee, over five hundred dollars a month, but they've got a pool, jacuzzi, pickleball court, library, you name it. I might go there myself, if it wouldn't make my commute worse. Besides, I'd have to sell my house to afford it, and we just don't have that kind of time.

"What if I bought it?" The coincidence of driving by the place, wanting to get out of the family home, and Deb's mom needing to move was almost too much to believe. It had to be some kind of kismet—one more piece of the universe telling her she needed a big change.

"What are you talking about?" Deb's wine glass hit the bar with too much force and sent a few red droplets flying onto the bar top.

"Is everything okay here, ladies?"

"Yes. We're totally fine." Lacey shooed the bartender away while she thought about her offer. It would help her friend out of a bind. But also, she didn't want to live in the big family home another day. She probably hadn't wanted to live there for years, she'd just been too busy to notice.

After Zach left for college, she'd thought about downsizing but figured he might want to come home to see his friends. Plus, it seemed like so much work to get rid of most of their stuff. She honestly hadn't thought about it since. Suddenly, making a clean break from the past seemed like a huge opportunity to reset her life. Maybe planning should take a back seat, and she should leap at this sudden opportunity.

"Let me look at your mom's place before you put it on the market. Go ahead and meet with the realtor and get a price, but don't sign anything. If I like it, and the price is reasonable, let's talk. It might be the perfect solution for both of us."

"But how? We're looking to close as soon as possible." Deb seemed incredulous.

"I can make it work."

"Well, if you're sure. Why don't you come over on Saturday after I meet with the realtor?"

"Deal." Lacey clinked her glass against Deb's. Some deep responsibility unhitched itself from her shoulders and floated away. She didn't have to worry about a job, or being a mom, or taking care of a big house. Soon, she might not have to worry about anything at all, except what to do with herself, and surely she'd figure that out. She could live a completely different life. And she'd earned it.

Chapter 3

Thirty days later, Lacey sipped a slushy margarita on the patio of her favorite Mexican restaurant and basked in the warm California sun. She sat at the head of a long table, and over fifty people lounged on the patio at her going away party.

Her assistant, Michele, had done a wonderful job organizing everything. Lacey hadn't wanted one of those dour affairs in a training room featuring grocery store cookies and cakes and a microphone that would lure every executive to the podium to thank her while puffing up their own worth. Nope. Happy hour was her happy place, and it made sense to end her career here.

Now Michele sat beside her, tears leaking out of her eyes. Lacey patted her hand. "You're going to be fine. You are an incredible administrative assistant and an asset to the company. Everyone knows that."

"But they haven't announced your replacement yet. Who knows what they'll do? I'm going to miss you so much." Michele's face grew splotchy.

"It'll be fine. They'll probably decide something soon." Of course, they wouldn't. They didn't think her internal recommendation had enough experience, so they'd opened a recruitment. She'd updated the job description, but her superiors still haggled over what they thought the position entailed. Yesterday, Justin had come to her and begged her to stay on as a consultant, at an exorbitant salary, until they had someone else on board. Saying no had been the most extraordinarily powerful moment of her career.

He looked like a lost child after that, but she didn't give a damn. First, they decided she wasn't right for the job and offered to buy her out. Then they wouldn't take her advice on who to hire or even what her job included. Screw them.

She hated leaving the rest of the department in the lurch, but with Justin and Bob above her, the recruitment would surely fail. They'd hire some twelve-year-old for ten bucks an hour and then watch as project productivity crashed company wide, costing far more than they'd save by letting her go.

Her eyes landed on Justin across the patio. The little rat sipped what looked like a Shirley Temple. He'd thought himself a wunderkind, someone whose ideas would transform the company through increased productivity and slashed costs. But his lack of experience, or even a basic understanding of how project management supported the business, had made her life hell and might bring the company to its knees.

It surprised her that her rage didn't light him on fire. She closed her eyes. *Be grateful*. Without him, she'd face more years in a job that hadn't brought her joy in far too long.

Michele grabbed her arm and pointed. Lacey's eyes followed her finger. She couldn't believe it. Maddie and Zach! Lacey jumped up and rushed to intercept them.

"Kids! What are you doing here?"

"We wouldn't miss your going away party," Maddie said, wrapping her in a hug.

"How did you even know?" Lacey released her daughter and turned toward her son.

"Michele told us," Maddie said, as Zach embraced her.

"This is the best surprise ever." She led them to the table and rearranged a few people so they could sit near her. She also gave Michele a giant hug and a whispered thank you. Lacey would miss this woman who knew her better than she knew herself. She wished she could take Michele with her to fill the gaping holes in her future the way she'd filled her daily calendar. But she didn't want to think about that now.

"How long are you staying?" Lacey asked her kids.

"Through the weekend," they answered simultaneously.

"Wonderful. You can help me pack up the rest of the stuff and decide what you want to keep from your old bedrooms."

"What are you talking about?" Zach asked. Maddie looked at her dumbfounded.

"I've sold the house. Don't worry, I haven't done anything with your stuff. I'll store it until I move into my new place." She should have told them, but the last few weeks had been a whirlwind, what with wrapping up work and getting the house ready to put on the market.

She'd had multiple bidders on the first day. Then she worked with the banks and a real estate agent to sign a contract and put money into escrow to purchase Deb's mom's condo in Ocean View Estates. There hadn't been time to tell the kids. Or maybe she'd been afraid they wouldn't want her to move. What they saw as their childhood home had become a burden weighing her down and keeping her from starting the rest of her life. At least she told herself that. She still had no idea what the rest of her life actually entailed.

"You've sold the house?" Maddie shook her head, then signaled the server. "I'll have a margarita and an extra shot of tequila," she said when the young blond waitress approached. The woman wore an embroidered skirt and blouse meant to approximate traditional Mexican attire, even though she looked like a college kid from Kansas.

Lacey turned her attention away from the waitress and back to her daughter. "I did. I hope you're not upset."

Maddie looked upset. "I guess not, but it seems kind of sudden."

"Where are you going to live?" Zach asked. "And did you keep my baseball cards?"

"The baseball cards are in a specially labeled box. I know they mean a lot to you. And I'm purchasing a much smaller condo." Only Deb knew about its location in a fifty-five plus development. Even though the people she worked with knew her age, moving into a retirement community seemed a little like giving up.

"I also plan to travel, finally." Not that she'd planned anything.

"That's great for you," Zach said. "Hey, did you ever move your money to a better bank? I assume you'll make a profit on the house."

The kids had talked to Lacey about this before, but no, she hadn't opened an account in a bank that had divested from fossil fuels to fight climate change. She told them she'd look into switching banks a year ago but never found the time.

"Maybe you can help me with that while you're here," Lacey offered.

"That'd be awesome. Also, there are some amazing nonprofits out there doing things like battling climate change or fighting for social justice. If you need something to do, maybe you could volunteer or even make a donation."

Her idealistic son's community work made her proud and worried her. Especially when he participated in rallies that antagonized the police. She didn't want him ending up in jail, or worse.

"Your mom has worked extremely hard for her money." Michele jumped into the conversation. "She deserves the chance to enjoy it. You don't know what she's put up with over the years."

A sheen of embarrassment spread across Lacey at Michele's fervor, but the woman made a good point. Lacey had put up with a lot of crap over thirty-eight years in the workforce. Sexism, misogyny, nepotism, minor harassment. In her younger years, she'd have sworn the world had changed and the need for strident feminism had passed. Unfortunately, the longer she worked, the more she experienced the entrenched patriarchy in action. And she had it easy compared to women of color and many others. That her kids would likely live through the same thing astounded her. The world should have progressed beyond this. Yet one more reason to leave that world behind.

"Oh, we know how hard she's worked," Maddie said.

A pang of guilt cut through Lacey. Maddie had regularly attended after-school programs and summer camps because she had a working mother. Especially after her ex moved back to Texas. Lacey lived the working mom's dilemma: tormented about spending too little time with her kids and riddled with guilt for not spending enough time at work.

"But that doesn't mean she can't contribute to worthwhile causes." Maddie stared her mother down.

"There are lots of nonprofits I donate to," Lacey said, needing to defend herself. "I give to an organization that builds libraries for kids around the world and another that invests in international microloans."

"Those are great causes, Mom. But there are lots of issues here at home as well." This time Zach broke in.

"But I contribute locally also. I belong to the lagoon foundation, the botanic garden, and two art museums." Lacey felt like a girl scout trying to earn badges for her good deeds. Kids today could be so frustrating. They wanted so much from their parents. Lacey hadn't really cared about what her mom did later in life. It truly didn't affect her.

"Those are all laudable issues," Maddie said. "But I think Zach is just trying to say that there are even more ways to contribute. Whether it's with money, or with time now that you're retired, the world needs you."

The words sank through Lacey like a stone. She didn't want to be needed anymore. Her kids didn't understand how she'd struggled to set them up so things might be a little easier for them. They hadn't worked their way through college the way she did. Although they did their part, one attending a state university and the other earning a scholarship.

She might have preferred to stay home, like many of the women on their block. Instead, she did her duty, and now she'd earned her reward. If only they could see that and let her live out the rest of her days free from responsibility.

"It's not like selling the house was a windfall," Lacey said. "I've paid that expensive mortgage every month for over twenty years. No one is giving me money. Also, I plan on living a long time and need that investment unless you're planning on taking me in."

In her mind, the comment had a teasing tone, but it came out angrier than she expected. Both kids looked suitably cowed. Maybe she'd gone too far or been a little too loud, especially given the looks people gave her from further down the table. Screw them. She never had to see any of them again after tonight.

"Mom." Zach reached across his sister and wrapped his warm hand around her wrist. "You haven't done anything wrong, and I didn't mean to make you upset. I just thought you might want to think about it."

Lacey put on her cheeriest smile. "I know, honey. Let's talk about it later. I want to enjoy my party."

Lacey steered the Prius off the Coast Highway and began the climb to the Torrey Pines hiking trails. Zach sat beside her while Maddie held her phone to her ear in the back seat.

"Thanks for bringing us up here, Mom. It's been years, and this is an important natural area," Zach said as she pulled into a parking space.

"I agree. It's also nice to see more walking and biking trails in North County," Maddie said after hanging up her phone. "By the way, Chuck says hi."

"That man is a keeper," Lacey said, glancing at Maddie in the rearview mirror just in time to see her daughter roll her eyes. Maddie had always hated Lacey commenting on her love life. Before Chuck, Lacey had rarely muttered anything positive about the string of boyfriends she'd met, including the one who always smelled like pot and the one who left Maddie crying after he cheated. With Chuck, Maddie had found someone as smart and driven as she was.

"Hey, let's change the subject," Zach said. He'd always played the buffer between Maddie and Lacey. "Are you involved with any of the environmental organizations down here?"

"Yes. I donate to the Batiquitos Lagoon Foundation, and I've been on their fun run several times." Lacey considered herself an environmentalist, always had.

"No, I mean have you ever volunteered?" Zach hauled his lanky frame out of the car.

"No, Zach. I've had a job. Remember. The job that helped put you through college." She slammed the door of the Prius with a little more gusto than necessary.

"Don't get upset, Mom." Maddie pulled her ponytail through the back opening of a baseball cap as she spoke. "We think it's awesome that you're retiring and would love to see you get involved in some meaningful causes. There are organizations that could use someone with your business experience."

"Yeah," Zach said. "Honestly, nonprofits rarely excel in project management."

Maddie took her turn in the *what should Mom do next* volley. "Besides, I know you. There's no way you'll be content staying at home all day. You're the busiest person I've ever met."

"I used to be busy because I had to be."

Lacey sighed and headed toward the trail. Whenever she spent time with her kids these last few years, they'd urged her to get involved. While she'd donated to a few organizations, she hadn't had time to give. Now that she'd finally retired after so many years of busting her butt, she had time. But she'd earned this time and wanted to spend it on herself, even if she didn't know how just yet.

"The last thing I want to do is work until I'm dead, and that includes giving away my time for free. Haven't I done enough?" She hated the whiny tone in her voice and hoped her kids hadn't picked up on it.

She carved her way down the dirt trail and out of the magnificent pines onto a sandstone cliff jutting toward the ocean. The orange dirt wound between scrubby plants before disappearing into a series of switchbacks leading to the beach below. Ahead of her, the vista opened to the deep blue Pacific topped by a topaz sky. She could see forever.

The ocean breeze tousled her hair and smelled like a voyage waiting to happen. The water pulled at her. Far out of sight lay the South Pacific, Asia, Australia. She'd read an article on Japan recently that made her want to visit the far-off islands. She looked to her left, certain the island on the horizon occupied Mexican waters, another country she'd always wanted to explore in depth. To her right lay the rest of California, then the Pacific Northwest, Canada, and Alaska. She'd longed to cruise through the Inside Passage up to where Alaska's glaciers met the ocean. She'd see pods of orcas and dolphins playing in the ship's wake. Longing for adventure thrummed in her chest.

She'd come from a generation where work meant everything. *What do you do?* had been the first thing she'd asked anyone she met. Her working hours extended late into the night after the kids went to bed. On weekends and holidays, she'd log in from swim or soccer practice, proud her boss would see emails time-stamped at eleven p.m. or on the Fourth of July. That's how she'd gotten ahead at work. Although it was never quite enough for the VP-level position she desired. But that race, with all its striving, had ended. Time for something new. Her view returned to the Pacific. She deserved an adventure, not working for free, not spending time alone in her home. She hated the guilt coursing through her, whispering for her to give more.

The kids came up behind her. Maddie wrapped an arm around her and gave her a squeeze. "We're not trying to harass you. We just think you have a lot to give."

"Well, I think it's time to enjoy myself. I want to travel, to seek adventure. I never got the chance to do that. First, I raised you two while working, and more recently, I had to focus on my job. I had a ton of responsibility, and the company depended on me to deliver. I always did." *Let that be enough.* She wanted to shout the words, but swallowed them instead, certain her kids would have preferred a mom who worked less and spent more time with them.

"I think that's awesome," Zach said. "You should take some time for yourself. You can come stay with me if you'd like."

His words made her want to set off on a never-ending cruise around the world. She giggled at the thought. She'd read about people who retired onto cruise ships. Maybe she'd look into that. If she didn't, it sounded like her kids would put her to work. And she'd already had a lifetime of that.

Chapter 4

By the time her kids left, Lacey had begun looking into retirement cruise ships. Maddie and Zach spoke constantly about a world on fire with racism, cruelty, and climate change. Perhaps they hadn't meant to make guilt crawl across her skin, but it had. It remained there still.

Of course, she knew about climate change and the ongoing wars and police brutality. Hadn't she done her part to combat it? She'd worn a yellow shirt with the other moms to protect young protestors. Of course, the worst she'd dealt with was a smoke bomb thrown toward them by a throng of middle-aged white people sporting American flags. As if free speech and protests weren't the heart of American democracy.

And she'd always tried to promote women and minorities at work. She understood the importance of their voices in a company whose products served everyone. She'd even advocated for blind resume reviews, where those reviewing resumes wouldn't see a candidate's names or photos, helping to prevent decisions based on unconscious bias.

But her kids acted like she was part of the problem. And sadly, every dilemma they brought up had worsened in her lifetime. It filled her with guilt just when she should be free from responsibility.

Besides, she didn't need her kids to tell her about global warming or crazier weather. She'd seen it. Fires in California had worsened, droughts in the West devastated habitats and sent water prices skyrocketing. But she always voted pro-green and had been one of the first people on her street to get solar panels. She, as an individual, had tried her best. And things got worse anyway.

It was almost a relief to drop the kids off at the train station. She'd offered to buy them plane tickets. When they told her their train tickets cost more than the flight, it flabbergasted her. Why spend over thirteen hours on a train when an airplane could get you there in less than two? Carbon emissions. Of course.

"Come visit us in San Francisco. You can stay with me in my apartment." Maddie's genuine offer touched Lacey, but a single weekend of guilt about the world she'd bequeathed to her children had depressed her.

It was time to start her new life. After all, she'd worked her whole life to take care of them. Of course she didn't want to leave her children with a planet on fire, but she still had her own life to live.

"I'd love to, honey, but I've got to wrap up this home sale, and then I'd like to take a little time off to see the world."

Zach sighed heavily, cementing her guilt. How could she love them so much and still very much want them to get on that train back to their regular lives?

"You two are the most incredible kids. I'm so proud of how you're dedicating your lives to making the world a better place." She remembered that feeling, the one where she'd brought new technology to the everyday world. In her early career, she'd spent each day at the forefront of a massive change for the better. New, computer-based technologies drove efficiencies and productivity up while costs fell.

But had anyone other than shareholders and the highest-level executives gained anything in the long run? It wasn't a question worth asking. Her time as a contributor had ended. She hugged each grown child, then waved when the train pulled away.

Monday morning came, and for the first time since she could remember, Lacey had no list of things to achieve. Claustrophobic emptiness gutted her, but she battled it with planning, her weapon of choice.

She would close on the family home in three weeks and buy Deb's mom's place two days later, although she'd already signed all the paperwork. She'd gone through the house with the kids and sorted everything into trash, donate, and keep piles. The kids had taken some of the keep items on the train, and the others she'd drop off at the post office. Then she'd move the rest to storage.

After she'd dealt with the physical baggage, she'd plan her future. Thinking about what she wanted from the rest of her life made her briefly miss the kids. Maybe someday she'd move closer to help when they had their own families. She'd often dreamed of having that kind of help when raising them on her own, but her parents only came to California for Thanksgiving and graduations.

And her children didn't need her yet anyway. Maddie had dated Chuck for a year and a half. Lacey expected them to get engaged at some point, although they didn't seem to be in any hurry. Zach apparently had a new boyfriend every few months. Someday he'd be speared by love, but it hadn't happened yet.

Thinking about love before she'd even made coffee caused her to want to loll in bed all morning. She needed more sex in her future. If only she had someone to share the lazy morning with—that would be something fun to do. For several years after the kids went to college, she'd had a casual relationship with a recently divorced neighbor. He'd excelled in bed. One night, she'd slept over after an evening of Netflix and a couple of bottles of wine. He'd woken in the morning raring to go, and despite morning breath and a mild headache, it had been the best sex of her life.

Eventually, his job took him to another city. Lacey heard through other neighbors that he'd remarried. He seemed like the kind of guy who'd do better with a wife, something Lacey hoped never to be again. But she'd been more than happy as the rebound girl.

If he'd still lived down the street, she'd have called him over to satisfy her needs. That's another thing a cruise ship might do, provide a revolving door of men with no strings attached. She'd watched *The Love Boat* as a child.

While she hadn't been on a cruise before, it seemed like the perfect balance of her own space and a place to meet new people. Fantasies of sitting at the captain's table with Merrill Stubing and finding a new on-ship romance every week flitted through her head.

She slid her iPad off the nightstand and typed in *cruise + retirement*. One article led to another and then to another. She found so many pluses: meals, a private room, and maids, not to mention lectures, performances, pools, and hot tubs—all while seeing the world. They even did your laundry. It sounded like paradise.

Once she'd started down the path, her project management expertise took over. Planning the next steps became easier than asking herself what she really wanted out of life.

She'd start with a cruise. Then, maybe she'd book the entire year or look into purchasing an apartment on a ship.

She found it hardest to choose a destination. She'd looked into cruising to Hawaii or Japan, the places she'd dreamed about when staring over the cliffs at Torrey Pines. But taking a cruise that far seemed more about seeing the ocean than the world.

She also wanted to visit places she'd never been, which took Hawaii off the list. She looked into Italy. After all, who didn't love Italian food? But so many websites said to avoid Italy in August.

Then she hit on Norway. Deb had been there with her family and raved about it. She found the website of a company whose ships traveled up and down the coast, stopping at most of the little towns along the water. In addition to watching the beautiful coast float by, she could learn to make gravlax, go on cultural tours, hike up a mountain, and sea kayak. She could even visit the world's northernmost brewery. Why the hell not? This was just the adventure she'd been looking for, and they had great prices left on the two-week voyage. She purchased the ticket before she could talk herself out of it.

Maybe she'd end up selling Deb's mom's place and buying a permanent berth on a ship. If not, the condo would become home. For once in her life, she would leave her worries and guilt behind and live the adventure of her dreams.

But even as she pushed the button to purchase her ticket, she wondered whether her rash decision signaled running toward the future or running away from bigger decisions about who she was and who she should be in this next phase of life.

Chapter 5

As the plane dropped toward Bodø, Norway, Lacey couldn't believe the pilot intended on landing. Nothing but gray surrounded them. They'd fallen through clouds for far too long.

Finally, she saw shapes outside. Bodies of water glowed silver against the gray clouds, and tree-topped hills rose beneath her. Drops of water splattered the window, and everything below looked slick and wet. They flew briefly over roadways and buildings and landed quickly.

The airport spit her out into savage rain, soaking her before she made it into the taxi. She prayed the hotel would have a room available even though she'd arrived before check-in. The airfield sprawled across a narrow peninsula. The town looked walkable, and despite the rain, she wanted to get out and explore after so many hours in the air.

She paid for the cab and rolled her suitcase and attached carryon into the hotel lobby. The modern space felt homey and exciting at the same time. Charcoal tiles and wood paneling lent a warm feel, as did the leather benches surrounding an open fire pit. Chrome pendant lights and Scandinavian furniture added modern décor to the hotel.

Even better, they checked her in and gave her a room key. She opened the door to her room and a wall of windows confronted her. The view overlooked the port where her ship would come in.

Her exhaustion melted away, and she jumped into the shower, then dressed for a rainy day. She explored the waterfront path into town, grateful the rain had gone from downpour to consistent, but no longer dramatic.

She'd planned on purchasing tickets for an ocean raft tour of the maelstrom, a huge whirlpool that formed in the local waters. Back in California, she'd decided traveling out to see such a wonder in an open rubber boat should kick off her exciting new life. Here, on a cold and rainy summer day, Lacey changed her plan.

She ducked into an adorable building with fish painted on it and found herself in the salmon center. The quasi museum focused on one of Norway's most important resources. The space had children's activities, displays, and a repeating movie about how climate change affected the Norwegian salmon industry. It was her kids all over again.

She escaped and hit the streets, wandering up one and down another. She hadn't eaten in hours and searched for a restaurant. Unfortunately, all the cute street side cafes had long lines of people waiting in the rain. The drops increased in tempo and volume as they hit the umbrella she'd picked up in the hotel lobby, and she worried about a coming deluge.

She found what looked like a small, two-story indoor mall and dashed inside before the worst of the rain hit. A loud cheer came from the interior of the building. She investigated and found a roomy pub down a walkway. One glance at an A-framed sign with a hamburger drawn on it, and she strode inside. Seemingly half the male population of Norway watched soccer at the bar.

Despite the crowd, a friendly young woman led her to a cozy booth that remained empty because it lacked a view of the TV. She asked if soccer games were always so popular, and after a confused look from the hostess, asked again using the term football. That's when she learned she'd arrived in time for the European championship, and Norway had made it to today's quarter final. Just then, the crowd released a chorus of groans as France tied Norway.

Lacey pulled out her phone and immersed herself in home and family. When her burger arrived, she scarfed it down as if she hadn't eaten in weeks. She sipped a beer and surreptitiously spied on the football fans, trying to shake off the loser feeling of dining alone.

Norway definitely had a type. Mostly blond, broad, and tall, the men had large hands and ruddy cheeks, perhaps from the beer. She caught a couple of them looking her way as she peeked around the booth. Most quickly shifted their gaze, although one smiled at her.

She wanted a life of travel, and she didn't have a partner. That meant putting herself out there to meet people when she could, and dining alone when she couldn't. If she didn't teach herself to enjoy the experience, this wouldn't work.

She ordered a second beer, to practice being alone and to delay returning to the bad weather. Soon, the game on TV ended, and the men filed out of the bar. The effects of the transcontinental trip weighed on her, dragging at her body and thoughts until she caught herself wanting to stretch out on the bench and nap.

Lacey had read she should power through jet lag so her body would adjust quickly to the new time zone. The advice seemed laughable as she sat in a cozy booth with two beers in her belly. She paid and made her way back to the hotel for a nap.

Her first foray into a foreign land challenged her, but she found plenty to enjoy. Despite the fatigue, a current of electricity sparked as the next phase of her life surged toward her.

Lacey woke to a gray world growing dark. Outside her picture window, the rain had let up, but the once pewter clouds had turned to lead. The blue had leached from the water and become yet another shade of gray. She grabbed her phone. How could it already be ten thirty at night?

She wanted more than the solitude of this gray world, so she fixed her hair and makeup and took the elevator to the ground floor. Warm and boisterous, the lobby seemed to turn back time to an earlier hour. People dined in the restaurant and drank at a raised bar.

She made her way up to the bar. Sitting on a stool overlooking three young men making drinks, she tried for a sophisticated, not lonely, vibe.

A gorgeous blond bartender approached. Lacey gave him a broad smile.

"What is Norway's most popular drink?" she asked.

"Aquavit. Would you like to try it?"

"Certainly." Of course she would. She'd promised herself to be brave, to push herself into new adventures and learn about the world and the people in it.

The man set a shot glass in front of her and filled it almost to the brim with a clear liquid. She wanted to ask whether to sip it or shoot it, but he'd already retreated down the bar. She picked up the glass and examined it. The liquid glowed orange from the firepit below, with a dash of neon blue thrown in from the bar lighting.

She took a large sip, figuring drinking half the aquavit would be appropriate regardless of tradition. It lit her esophagus on fire. She gasped for air, sending flames through her nose and throat. Tears escaped her eyes, perhaps to douse the flames that had already made their way into her gut and twisted it with a sharp pang. What the hell was this stuff?

She slammed the glass back on the bar. Aquavit splashed everywhere, the bar, her hand, her clothes. She inhaled again. Air hit her scraped-clean nasal passages like ice. Lacey had never so vehemently hated a drink.

"Are you alright?" a different bartender asked.

Lacey struggled to see him through her tears. "I don't think that's my drink." She'd just as soon chug isopropyl alcohol straight from a bottle. It probably wouldn't taste any different.

"Ah, yes. It is very strong. Perhaps you would like a cider or a fruit beer?"

She'd like her lungs and internal organs repaired, but he didn't have that on offer. Fruit beer sounded too weird, and she'd had enough experimentation. "I'll have a cider, please. And a glass of water."

The cider tasted fine, at least what she could perceive of it with her destroyed tastebuds. She noticed an elegant man down the counter from her. Her age, he seemed to have an excellent skin care routine and manicured nails. His auburn sweater paired perfectly with a camel jacket. He sipped what looked exactly like her aquavit with no side effects whatsoever. It astounded her.

The bartender set a long rectangular plate in front of him. On it were rounds of toast covered by lox, cream cheese, and capers. It looked divine.

"I'll have what he's having," she said to the bartender the next time he checked on her.

"Ah, gravlax, another Norwegian specialty."

That almost scared her off, but she told herself to be bold. Soon she had her own plate. She reached for a toast and sniffed it before taking a bite. Just in case.

This time, it was exactly what she'd expected, only better. The flavorful salmon had hints of mustard and dill, and the cream had just the perfect amount of sour to pair with the fish. She devoured it. She had to keep trying new things. It might not always work out, but sometimes it would be fabulous.

Lacey woke at three thirty in the morning, her sleep schedule irrevocably askew. When she turned to the big picture window, the clouds had cleared, and the world seemed to glow. Night had fallen, even here above the Artic Circle, but unlike at home, the sky wasn't black enough to show the stars beyond. She could also see farther than should have been possible. The details of the dock and snow-capped mountains far in the background became clear as if each object had become its own source of light.

She'd heard about the midnight sun but had missed that by over six weeks. She scooted toward the windows and pulled the thick down comforter around her. Everything in this world seemed different from the places she'd left at home. She let the years of work fall from her consciousness, let worries about money and her future drop to the floor, let go of every problem, and sat in the beautiful moment.

After an unknown period of time, apricot streaks crept into the near-dark world, then the palest shimmery pink. As dawn began its early break, a giant boat glided into view, barely ruffling the smooth water. The ship contained three horizontal stripes. The lowest matched the deep navy of the water. A bright red stripe divided the blue from white paint above. She counted seven levels, maybe eight. When the boat swung around to the side, she saw its name. This was the vessel that would whisk her into her future.

A thrum of excitement coursed through her veins. She didn't need to be on the boat for well over an hour, but she dressed and headed out of the hotel in fifteen minutes. She couldn't wait for the rest of her life to begin.

The harbor smelled like tangy salt and excitement. Strong dock workers loaded goods onto the ship. She found a ramp and lugged her giant suitcase up it, over the threshold, and into the boat. She was home.

In a nook to one side, an attendant waited to check her in, just like in a hotel. The smiling blond woman asked if she'd like to upgrade to a room three floors higher for two hundred dollars for the entire trip. Lacey immediately said yes. Then she took an elevator to her floor.

The tiny room had a small sofa on one side and a pull-down bed on the other. The entire bathroom would have fit in her Carlsbad shower. But this room was hers, all hers, for the duration of the trip. She peered out the porthole window and saw the hotel where she'd spent the night.

Excitement tumbled through her. She wanted to document this new journey, the reward that her years of labor had bought. Pulling out her phone, she took a picture of the hotel through the window. Then she photographed her new living space. She wanted a picture of the outside of the ship as well. The boat wouldn't leave for an hour yet, so she went back down the elevator, snapped a photo of the check-in nook, and then retreated down the gangplank, alight with excitement.

The size of the ship made it hard to get the entire thing in the frame. She wished she'd taken a picture from her hotel room. If she hurried, she could go back to the hotel and take one from the lobby, but she didn't want to go backwards. This trip was about moving forward into whatever was next in her life. She could hardly wait to discover what that was.

A line of people now waited to board the ship. A man with gray swept-back hair left the line and rolled his suitcase toward her.

"Would you like me to take a photograph of you and the ship?" he asked. He had an accent, although she couldn't place it.

"I would love that. Thank you." Lacey handed him her phone.

He took several photos of her and the vessel from different angles, and she made sure he got a shot that included the ship's name. Proof the next phase of her life had started. She thanked him repeatedly as she reclaimed her phone.

"Of course," he said. "You are American, right?"

"Yes, freshly arrived. Where are you from?"

"I am from Austria. This is my first time on the *Hurtigruten*, but I hear it is wonderful."

"I've never even been on a cruise ship before. I'm so excited." She sounded ridiculous, like a kid who just unwrapped their favorite Christmas present. She reveled in the feeling and wished it would last forever.

They returned to the gangplank, and he introduced himself as Alexander. Lacey also met his wife, Marie. The couple checked in while Lacey left to tour the ship.

The boat seemed never-ending. No wonder people retired onto cruise ships, and this wasn't even a massive one. On one of several main levels, she found two fast food type joints and a convenience store. The ship had a library, a fancy restaurant, and a bar. There were sitting areas along the ship's sides, and she discovered a door that led to a large open deck with a stack of lounge chairs. While the sky had cleared, lounging in a bathing suit wouldn't happen in this chilly air.

On a different floor, she found the main restaurant which served buffet style meals. It wouldn't open for a couple of hours, but it already smelled divine. Exploring further, she discovered a weight room and an enormous sauna. That, she might have to try.

She continued toward the front of the ship, the bow, as she recalled. There, she found a magnificent room with glass walls showing a panoramic view of the coast. Cozy sitting areas on several levels were interspersed with long benches and tables for two. Empty at this hour, the space looked like it had something akin to a bar toward the back of the large room. Lacey approached, drawn by the smell of coffee.

Three large coffee dispensers along with ceramic mugs waited for her on the counter. With a steaming cup of java in her hands, she located a spot on a plush bench at the highest level in the very front of the room and looked out over Bodø.

How did one measure a life? Lacey had assessed employees, and been evaluated herself, on productivity, personality, and anything else the company desired. She excelled at productivity. She could get more done in less time than almost anyone she'd ever worked with. It had won her prizes: promotions, raises, great reviews.

Now that she had exited the hamster wheel, how should she measure her time, her life? Number of books read? Number of miles traveled?

She closed her eyes. She just wanted to stop. Retiring might mean becoming a whole new person, one who enjoyed things instead of measuring them. She relaxed into the fabric of the bench and let the steam from the coffee warm her face.

It sounded so easy, but something in her boiled for attention. She missed throwing herself into a project to see what she could accomplish. She had become a person with her switch stuck in the *on* position. It had never seemed like a bad thing before.

Part of her wanted to get out a notebook and create a plan for how *Lacey would learn to relax and love retirement*. But that was the problem. She had days in front of her with no set plan, nothing to do. For a brief second, she wondered how she would survive.

Then she shook her head out of her ridiculous melancholy. This was just a transition to something new. She'd be fine.

She pulled out her phone and looked through the photos Alexander had taken. The best one she sent to Maddie and Zach. She half wished they were here with her. It would be fun to go on vacation with them again. They'd turned into such interesting people.

The ship's horn shocked her. Did the people in the town grumble about the loud noise so early in the morning? Perhaps they used it as an alarm clock. It sounded again, and then the ship started moving. Lacey sat, transfixed, as the coastline swept by and she sailed into the future.

Chapter 6

Lacey stayed in the viewing room for hours. Other people came in, lots of older couples, a few families. She refilled her coffee cup several times, smiled at a few people. A group of five sat right below her at a table. They had British accents and talked about the types of birds they wanted to see on the trip.

She had never studied people the way she did now. She asked herself who she'd like to have a conversation with and get to know better. And how did one initiate that? If she didn't have people to talk with, to form relationships with, no matter how short, then this life wasn't for her.

The questions dragged her down. She didn't want to think so hard on the first day of her cruise. Maybe she just needed to eat.

The breakfast buffet offered a plethora of choices. She reminded herself she didn't need to try everything on the first day. Even so, her plate overflowed with fresh fruit, two different types of hearty, seedy brown bread, an egg, a sausage patty, and a single slice of bacon.

She avoided the large tables set for four or six at the front of the restaurant and navigated to a table for two near a back corner. Maybe tomorrow she'd claim a larger table and see if anyone joined her like in middle school. Or perhaps she'd return to this table, perfectly situated for viewing the ship's patrons. She needed to grant herself a little grace while she figured out retirement.

To ensure she met more passengers, and to have fun, as soon as she finished breakfast she signed up for several excursions. Two fit and athletic young men, probably the youngest people on the ship, worked the activities counter. They told her about excursions to view eider geese, kayak around the Lofoten Islands, and prepare gravlax, as well as a series of hiking and bus tours.

Like at the breakfast buffet, she had a hard time deciding. Eventually, she chose the gravlax class, a whale watching tour, and a visit to a sheep farm. Her only hard no was the cod liver oil tasting.

Not knowing what else to do with herself, she returned to the viewing room and sat as close as she could to the window. The ship hugged the coast, and the craggy, verdant hills jutted up from the calm sea in the most interesting configurations. The early morning mists sometimes veiled her view, but other times she saw sheep grazing on hilltops. They glided past villages with brightly colored houses along the water's edge, and she wondered how people got to them. The towns seemed so isolated. She felt a little isolated herself.

She'd set up her life this way. Most of the people on the cruise seemed paired up. She'd seen a very old woman accompanied by what Lacey assumed was her daughter, but few single people.

She wanted the cruise, but didn't want a man, at least not a permanent one, hadn't for ages. Sure, she'd dated people over the years, but active children left scant time for dating. Besides, a serious relationship would have meant introducing someone to the kids. Because she didn't want to marry again, she refused to put them through that.

But her kids had been gone for years, despite her still using them as an excuse. She hadn't totally moved on with that part of her life. She'd hooked up with guys at conferences a time or two. No one had to worry about a relationship when everyone flew back to a different hometown when the conference ended.

Her affair with the man down the street had been her only serious fling since Sean, her ex, had left them. She shifted in her seat just thinking about the neighbor. That had been hot. But he'd sold the family house and moved to Los Angeles about a year into their affair. She'd never questioned trying to turn the relationship into something permanent. Honestly, he wasn't that interesting to talk to. But when he called and asked if she wanted to come over and watch a movie, she went every time. Sometimes they didn't even turn on the TV.

Lacey fanned herself and took a gulp of water, imagining his lips on her breasts, his scruffy cheek working its way down her belly. It must be the jet lag causing these feelings so early in the day. She needed to get back on a regular schedule.

"Lacey. There you are."

Lacey spun around at the sound of her name as if she'd been caught watching porn. Alexander waved at her as he pulled Marie in her direction.

"We've been looking for you. Have you had breakfast yet?" His voice seemed to boom across the room, interrupting her reverie. Not that she should have been having those thoughts in public.

"I have, and it was delicious."

"You must join us for dinner tonight. We don't want you to have to eat alone." She cringed as his loud voice announced her status to everyone in the room. Marie nodded beside him, her blond bob swinging beside her ears.

"That sounds lovely," Lacey said in almost a whisper. Hopefully, he'd get the message and lower his voice.

They plopped themselves down at her table. Alexander asked about her work, and Lacey responded in kind. A hint of dread went through her when Marie pulled a book out of her handbag and proceeded to ignore them. Would Lacey be stuck here all morning talking to this guy?

Fortunately, years in business had trained her beyond the submissive, feminine ways of dealing with men she'd learned as a child. The next time he stopped to take a breath, she made her move.

"It has been lovely speaking with you two. I'll see you tonight at dinner." Then she slipped away.

She wandered the ship again, beset with worry that maybe she didn't know how to *do* leisure. On the back deck, the lounge chairs remained stacked due to the chilly weather, but she stood at the railing and watched the world go by. The need for action overwhelmed her. Would she ever get used to the days stretching before her like this? Normally, she crammed her days with meetings, projects, emails, fires needing water, managing personalities. The world had narrowed to Lacey, a boat, and a beautiful shoreline. Was that enough?

She shook her head, refusing to put up with this negative attitude. Diagnosing herself with jetlag, she returned to her cabin. She'd brought a Kindle full of books she'd meant to read for years. She turned on the device, stretched out on the couch, and perused the selections.

She needed a book about a woman on an adventure. That would get her in the right mood for this trip. She found a memoir about a woman who had bicycled through South America. It was exactly the spirit of adventure she desired.

She woke hours later, her face smashed against the side of the couch and drool on her shirt. Still not fully awake, she made her way to the bathroom, stepping on her Kindle which had fallen to the floor. The screen cracked into a spider's web.

"Damn it," she yelled into empty air. Now what would she do during these forever-long days? She looked at her phone. Almost four in the afternoon. She'd slept for hours.

She attempted to shower in the tiny stall and ended up flooding the entire bathroom. What would go wrong next? She took a deep breath to calm herself. She'd asked for this life, had paid a lot of money for it.

Lacey vowed to make it work. She'd always appreciated a challenge. Even when it temporarily overwhelmed her.

Picking a shimmery aubergine skirt and cream sweater, she dressed for dinner. She'd return to the viewing room until then. She made up her face and checked herself in the mirror before she left the room. Not bad, although tomorrow she needed to hit the gym in order to survive the breakfast buffet.

She lodged herself near the glass in the viewing room. Through the giant window, steel gray water met mist so low it hugged the black shore. She shivered and wrapped her shawl tightly around her, despite the well-heated room. Focusing on her hands instead, she opened a book she'd found in the ship's library and transported herself to yet another different location.

"Hello. May I sit?"

Lacey jumped at the interruption. When she looked up, a ruddy man stared back at her. Hefty and tall, he forced her to lean back as he bent into her personal space.

"Do you speak English?" he asked.

"Yes. Can I help you?"

"I would like to sit down." Instead of waiting for permission, he lowered himself into the only other seat at the small table. Lacey glanced around. While fuller than when she'd arrived, the room still contained plenty of open seats.

"Thank you. I am Johan." He stuck his beefy hand toward her. "You are?"

Automatically she reached her hand toward his, then wished she hadn't as his sweaty palm touched hers. "Lacey. I was just reading."

"Are you here alone?" he asked.

Immediately, her alarm bells went off. "It's very nice to meet you, but I was enjoying my book and would like to get back to it." She hadn't dealt with corporate bullies for years without learning a few things. First, shut them down early.

"Ah. What book are you reading?"

Lacey cocked an eyebrow and crossed her arms, preparing to verbally annihilate the rude man. Just then, Alexander swooped down to her table.

"Lacey. I found you. Are you ready for dinner?"

"Yes." Lacey stood and followed Alexander to where Marie waited at the entrance to the viewing room. She didn't even glance at Johan as she left.

"Would you like to invite your friend?" Marie asked, and Lacey wondered at the enthusiasm in her voice.

"Definitely not." She appreciated being saved but would have preferred to fight her own battle. Now she felt she owed Alexander something, when really, she could have handled it.

Then she sighed and let it go. Not everything had to be a battle anymore. Hopefully, retirement had changed that.

They returned to the buffet, now decked out with sumptuous meats and chafing dishes. Alexander held court at the table, linking one tale to another about his business, hobbies, and topics about which he had strong opinions. Marie looked like she wanted to pull her book out of her purse. Lacey sure did.

She wanted a primer on how to meet the right people on a cruise. And how to avoid everyone else. Her encounters this evening reminded her there were worse things than being alone. Would she ever find balance on this ship?

The heavy meal hit her gut like a bowling ball, and she wished she'd opted for a pizza or sandwich at the café next to the convenience store on board. Next time.

She escaped by pleading jet lag. Back in her room, she changed into pajamas and turned out the lights. Through her small window, the misty world flowed by. She fully relaxed, something she probably hadn't done in years. There'd always been kids to worry about before, projects to complete, an endless list of errands she somehow found time to achieve. Now, no one needed her. She could sit in a tiny room on a giant ship on the other side of the world from her former obligations and just rest.

Lacey woke early again, hours before a morning tour of the sheep farm and island town she'd signed up for. Her excursion left just after breakfast when the boat docked at a small town that fringed the coast. Blue water, black rocky beaches, mountains painted in lush green grass. Had she stepped into a fairyland? The primary-colored houses, yellow, blue, and red, looked ready for a photo from the tourism bureau. So far, Norway did not disappoint. Everything appeared exactly as it had in the brochure. Although, it was a good thing the fishy smell hadn't translated onto paper.

Thirty people from the boat joined her on the tour. The fresh-faced guide herded them onto a tour bus. A woman took the seat beside Lacey and introduced herself as Angela, an attorney from London. When Lacey returned the introduction, the words project manager had half-escaped her mouth before she clamped her lips shut. "Retired," she said a second later. "Just."

Angela's husband had joined her on the cruise but had no desire to see a sheep farm. They struck up a conversation and stuck together like new friends as they toured the farm.

Fluffy white sheep grazed on green pastures, and the lambs danced around as if performing a show. "This is ridiculously beautiful." Lacey sighed, contentment at the state of the world flowing through her. Maybe she had figured this thing out.

"Indeed, it is lovely," Angela said. "It's a shame about how climate change is going to ruin this way of life."

Lacey turned to her, wondering if her daughter had suddenly taken on a British accent. "What do you mean?" she asked, although she really wanted to shout *please, no.*

"Norway is one of the countries most affected by climate change."

"Sea level rise?" Lacey knew from Maddie that islands and coasts would be hard hit.

Angela looked at her and shook her head. "No, actually. Because of where it's situated, Norway won't see as much sea level rise as nations near the equator. But the weather patterns will likely change more than other places. Less snow, more rain, the melting of the permafrost."

"How do you know all that?" Lacey couldn't have said why that question popped out. She'd prefer to end the conversation. But she was curious. Angela wasn't much younger than Lacey, but she spoke the way her daughter did.

"We're seeing change in England too. I'm a corporate barrister, and now the companies I work with must determine how to deal with the future. Climate change is a big part of that."

"I just don't understand how it all happened." Lacey couldn't keep the frustration from her voice. "Everyone in my generation was pro-environment. Well, that's not true. But so many of us cared." That was true. She had cared deeply. And she'd wanted to do something about it.

She had wanted to change the world once. Fresh out of college, she helped a business systems company in Dallas computerize their customers' offices. She'd adored helping companies move from physical files to online ones.

Her company had paid for her MBA, and the more she learned, the bigger the changes she implemented. From the beginning, she understood these systems would make an enormous difference in the nonprofit world. She cared about the environment, the burning of the Amazon, the hole in the ozone layer.

With her newly minted degree in hand, she mailed resumes and cover letters to a slew of nonprofits in Washington, DC, and San Francisco. She applied for office manager, IT, and tech positions and received nothing but rejections. Years later, she tried one more time, emailing her resume to a land trust and a conservancy group, both looking for project managers. By then, she'd done project management work for a decade for profit-minded corporations. She wanted to spend her life making a difference. She wasn't even granted an interview.

So now, why should she feel guilty? She'd tried. She'd wanted to make a difference, and they hadn't wanted her. Yet she still gave money to environmental organizations, despite the snub. How could climate change be her fault?

Lacey glanced at Angela as they walked into a bright red barn with white trim to watch the goat milking. Angela harped on about the environment. "We had the opportunity to stop climate change in the late seventies and early eighties. Unfortunately, the Reagan and Thatcher administrations tanked those efforts."

"Really?" Lacey knew some of this from Maddie, but this woman had lived through those times with an awareness Lacey didn't share. Perhaps she had some different insight.

"Oh, yes. The petroleum industry got to them. They knew more about climate change than anyone back then. They only started denying it when the governments got together to try to address the effects of global warming. After that, the petrol companies started a massive campaign of misinformation." Angela delivered the words in a matter-of-fact manner completely different from Maddie's passionate arguments.

Lacey trudged toward a wooden wall dividing them from the milking operation. She peeked over and saw six goats attached to a machine by their udders. "Christ, it reminds me of pumping."

Angela giggled beside her. "God, those were terrible days. My breasts were sore for six months."

Lacey cupped her own breasts in remembered pain. "It was barbaric. But we had to do it for their brain development. Now, of course, my kids are smarter than me."

"I hardly believe that." Angela paused for a minute. "May I ask you a question? What made you decide to retire?"

"A buyout of my position. I'd been waiting for it forever. I didn't hate my job or anything, but I'd been doing the same damn thing for so long. Besides, I've always dreamed about retirement. You know, the pot of gold at the end of the rainbow of hard work. I'm looking forward to relaxing, seeing the world, doing all the things I never had time for because I was working." Why did she need to overexplain her decision? She had earned her retirement.

They moved from the barn to the gift shop where small cups of cider and samples of cheese greeted them. Lacey bought her favorite cheese and a package of crackers. Maybe at the port she could buy a bottle of wine. It would make for a scrumptious dinner.

Back on the bus, Lacey continued her earlier conversation with Angela "When do you think you'll retire?"

"I'm not sure that I will, at least not for a long while yet. My career is getting more interesting now that I've shifted my work to environmental concerns. I can't imagine not working. What would I do all day, putter around in the garden?"

Guilt from Angela's statement landed squarely on Lacey's shoulders. Should she do more? She was still healthy, had a sharp mind. Sharper tongue. But damn it, she deserved retirement. She looked out the window where Kelly grass and slate hills pummeled her with their beauty and assured her she'd made the right decision. She never would have seen this if she hadn't retired, and she still had a whole world to explore.

Back in her cabin, Lacey dug into her research on cruise ship retirement. An almost frenetic energy pushed her to make a permanent decision about the rest of her life. She didn't want to be like Angela and work until she died. Even though Angela seemed entirely happy.

She'd had a great day meeting a new friend and exploring the shore. This kind of cruise ship life, she could handle. She almost put down a deposit on a ship where you purchased your cabin. Like a time share, the company would rent it to others when she left the boat to travel elsewhere. In the end, she couldn't do it.

She put a deposit down on another cruise instead, one that went from the west coast down to Mexico. She'd heard of people retiring to Mexico. Maybe she should cruise for a few months and see if she found an alluring place to spend the rest of her years. It was all so confusing. She couldn't stay in Carlsbad and just sit around. She'd never been a sit around type of person. That's why she'd gotten so far in her career. But she would never go back to work. That ship had sailed.

Chapter 7

Lacey woke up to the boat docking in the city of Trondheim. She'd become used to the small changes in momentum as the boat slowed or quickened as they approached or left a port. This would be her largest city in Norway yet, and she looked forward to exploring it. She'd decided against the tour and planned on taking off on her own.

She walked the half mile into town with the other passengers, then slipped down a side street while the others chatted in the main square. The boat had docked at six a.m. and the city lay quiet in the morning glow. She trudged up a street that skirted the city center and made her way toward a cathedral she wanted to visit.

She approached the building, whose many dark spires stretched to pierce the low-slung clouds. It had an eerie vibe and had likely birthed many scary stories. Her skin tingled as the path passed through an ancient looking cemetery. So many dead bodies. She stopped and debated whether her stroll disturbed the dead. No sounds reached her through the unreasonably quiet air.

She spun around and trotted back down the hill, some odd dread surfacing. She'd led a life remarkably free from death. Both her parents had lived past eighty. She tried to eat right, had taken short walks during the day, mostly to figure out problems at work, but it kept her moving. The morning chill and dark thoughts caused a shiver. How much time did she have left?

Twenty years. If she followed her parents, she'd have twenty good years, maybe a few more. Her first twenty years, she'd been a kid. Then she had ten working years, when she married and started a family. The next twenty, she'd split herself between work and raising children, barely finding time to breathe. And then the last ten, she'd toiled, striving to work harder and smarter so she'd reach her career aspirations.

A crack in the sidewalk caused her to stumble. She recovered, then wiped a tear from her cheek remembering how the company denied her a promotion. She'd applied for the Chief Information Officer job, an executive-level position, years earlier. Four years, to be exact. Same month, even. That she remembered the date so well stung almost as bad as the fact that they'd rejected her.

She'd been qualified. Overqualified. She'd actually handled the job in a temporary capacity for three months. The prior CIO had cleaned out his office and left with a day's notice after getting an offer at twice his salary. Lacey had carefully guided her career to this point. She attended the right conferences, earned the right certifications, put together training programs, had an article published in a professional journal.

And instead of promoting her, they moved Bob into the slot, a guy who probably had less than fifty percent of the qualifications listed in the job posting. Outraged, she'd burst into Julie's office.

"The CEO felt like he had to," Julie said. "Bob is totally screwing up the administrative services department. They have to get him out of there."

"But he doesn't know anything about IT or project management. Nothing." Lacey had managed to keep tears out of her eyes, but her wobbly voice betrayed her.

"Yes, but *you* do. Help him out a little. He won't be around forever. He's older than you and will likely retire soon."

"But it's not fair." She sounded like a whiny child.

"No, it's not. But you have a good job with great benefits. Stay. See what happens."

"I swear, Bob must have photos of the CEO fucking a goat," Lacey said, only half joking.

"They're friends from college. Bob has been here from day one."

At that, Lacey took a sick day and spiffed up her resume. Only no one wanted to hire a fifty-six-year-old woman. So, she stayed. And Bob, perhaps realizing his own incompetence, hired an assistant CIO. But did he choose her, the person keeping the department running despite his boneheaded business decisions? Of course not. He didn't want to hire a woman in her late fifties either. So, he hired a twenty-nine-year-old boy to be her manager.

Even on the other side of the world, the memory ached. Lacey swiped at the tears flooding down her face. She glanced around, thankful for the empty street. It was a ridiculous reason to cry.

Besides, she'd show them. She was free now. Free to live whatever kind of life she wanted. Free of the burden of ridiculous men so tied up in their own egos that they would sacrifice corporate goals and shareholder money just to keep the bro system in place.

Freedom. She'd earned it. Now she just needed to figure out how to spend it. She wished she could send those jackasses a photo of her enjoying her cruise. Maybe she'd send this year's Christmas card from her new home aboard a ship in an exotic location. That would show them.

The prospect of a life at sea, so far from her prior life, tied first to a man who had let her down and then a company that had done the same, sounded like something she should run toward. But was life on a ship an escape or a trap? She had so many competing emotions. If she had planned better, then maybe she wouldn't feel so lost. Ironic, coming from a project manager.

At the bottom of the hill, she turned away from town and stepped onto a bridge across an utterly still river. Peaked buildings in multiple hues lined the water, each at least five stories tall. They created a canyon, and the glasslike water reflected their images back to them. The peaceful scene calmed her nerves, but she still wondered why the city seemed empty. Nonetheless, she vowed to enjoy this excursion.

On the far side of the river, she found a quaint street lined with restaurants and shops. She needed a cup of coffee, wanted to see other people so she knew she was alive after her strange reaction to the graveyard. What was wrong with her? She had to quit thinking about death and job losses. Coffee. She needed coffee.

She found a cute yellow bakery with a signboard outside. When she spied people inside moving bread and pastries from place to place, it lifted her heart. The aroma of baked goods pulled her toward the door. Which was locked. She looked at the bakery hours, then looked at her phone. Still an hour before it opened. She almost started crying again.

Instead, she kept walking. Eventually, she came across a man who looked like he'd stepped out of the Gorton's Fisherman logo. He had gray hair, yellow overalls, and large hands coiling an enormous rope.

"Excuse me. Do you speak English?" she asked.

"Ya." He looked at her but didn't smile.

"Do you know why all the shops are closed?"

His eyebrows knitted for a moment. "It is Sunday. We had big parties last night. People are sleeping." With that, he turned his attention back to his rope.

Lacey stood there for a moment, hoping he'd look back up. Since he didn't seem like talking, she eventually moved on. She wandered toward the center of town. More people appeared, and when she saw a gathering down a side street, she headed toward it. Fortunately, she didn't recognize anyone from the ship in the half-dozen or so people gathered around a glass-fronted shop. The scent of coffee and fresh bread hit her before she could see inside. Her step quickened. Gilt letters scrawled Godt Brød across the door, and she opened it to a wave of heat and enticing aromas.

She ordered a latte and pointed to three different pastries. It seemed excessive, yet she'd barely narrowed down the selection to three.

She settled onto a stool at a bar that overlooked the bakery operations. Racks of bread rolled by, and occasionally ovens beeped, causing an employee to rush over, unload freshly baked loaves and reload the oven with racks of dough. A pink-cheeked woman handled the bread. Lacey imagined she rose early, worked hard, and returned home with a sense of satisfaction of a job well done. Lacey had been useful once.

She turned her focus to her pastries and took a bite of each one. The decadent treats immediately cured her melancholy. A Danish with a yellow center and a grainy muffin tasted like far better versions of their American equivalents. Her favorite looked like a cinnamon roll but had a far more complex flavor. Coffee and her sugar high made the world a little brighter.

She could have stayed all morning in the warmth and constant action of the bakery. However, the ship would leave without her. On her way out, she bought two freshly made sandwiches and a bag of granola. They would make a nice respite from the heavy food on the ship.

Along with baked goods, she decided to give herself a little grace. Changing your life in an instant was both rewarding and hard. She'd faced a rollercoaster of emotions in less than two hours.

If she applied her usual get-it-done attitude, instead of dwelling on past disappointments, she'd be fine. No more looking backward. Not when she had such an exciting future ahead. She returned to the giant ship, ready to fill her life with fresh experiences and brand new people.

"Lacey?" A man's shouting voice reached her as she walked up the ship's ramp.

She turned back toward the city. She couldn't place the voice, although it sounded familiar. Then she spied a man trotting toward her. Someone straight out of her past. What the hell was her ex-husband doing in Norway?

Lacey's shock glued her to the ramp, despite the people around her trying to get onboard. What weird coincidence was this?

"Sean. What are you doing here?" The question left her lips, but not loud enough for him to hear. She wanted to let herself drift into the ship's entry and pretend he wasn't bustling people out of the way to get to her.

Finally, she stepped as close as she could to the railing, giving others the chance to get by. Sean caught up to her and enveloped her in a hug. What the hell? She didn't hug him back, couldn't with her hands wrapped around her bakery bag.

"I'm so glad I found you. I've been waiting since before the ship docked. I'm not sure how you slipped by me." He sounded happy, eager to see her. Their meeting had not surprised him.

"What are you doing here?" Her brain lagged, unable to process him being here, on purpose.

"Well, the kids told me you'd decided to take a cruise, and I thought it sounded like a wonderful idea. Let's get off this ramp and go inside. I've already checked in." He gently tugged her arm toward the ship's opening.

"You booked a cabin?"

"Yes. Of course." He pulled at her again before turning to face her. "I can see this is a bit more of a surprise than I expected."

"I, I don't know what to say. I don't know why you're here." They hadn't seen each other in years, not since Zach's graduation. What did he want?

"Listen, the kids called. They said you were talking about spending the rest of your life on a cruise ship. It surprised me, and I wanted to make sure you were okay."

"The kids put you up to this?" That stretched her imagination even further. She'd been on her own since, well, since Sean left. She'd raised two kids, had a great career, and now people were acting like she needed checking up on because of how she wanted to retire. She didn't deserve this.

"I wouldn't say they put me up to it. They were just a little concerned, and I thought I'd check things out."

Anger flared in Lacey. "I've worked my whole fucking life. I've worked much harder than I would have if you'd stood by your commitment to our family. And now that I finally have the money and the time to do exactly what I want to do, you're suddenly here—overly concerned that I'm spending time on a cruise. What the hell is wrong with you?"

The last few stragglers on the ramp eyed them as they shuffled past, but Lacey didn't care. The fury that someone who'd run out on her years ago thought he could check up on her now blazed through her bones. What an ass.

Sean dropped his hand from her arm. "I forgot how much you hated surprises. I'm sorry."

The comment shocked her again. Sean had never been the type to say I'm sorry. She closed her mouth, which gaped open uncomfortably. "Well, let's not cause a scene. I suppose we should go inside." Lacey took a wobbly step up the ramp, her plans for the trip changed in an instant.

"It's lunchtime. How about I buy you a meal?" Sean looked cowed, like he feared she'd refuse.

Something in Lacey let loose. She couldn't change the situation, but she could roll with it. She didn't hate this man. He was the father of her children. And once, long, long ago, she'd loved him. He'd caught her off guard and shouldn't question her intentions, but the anger faded along with the shock.

"I just picked up a couple of sandwiches at a fantastic bakery in town. Why don't we meet in the viewing room and have a little lunch and talk? They've got a bar." Still stuffed from her breakfast pastries, she'd happily share the sandwiches. And she could use a stiff drink.

Chapter 8

Lacey told Sean she'd meet him in thirty minutes. While he picked up his suitcase from the front desk, she took advantage of an open elevator door to escape. Back in her room, she wanted to pace back and forth. Movement helped her think, but she could only go a few steps before having to turn around. She could have gone into the hallway, but she didn't want to risk seeing him.

With each minute that dragged by, her anger returned. Her emotions hadn't cycled like this since pregnancy. Thrilled to get away one moment, the next she'd sink almost into a depression about the past or wallow in an uncertain future. Seeing Sean had lit her with anger, then she'd thought perhaps it would be nice to have a friend on board.

But the last thing a sixty-year-old woman needed was someone checking up on her. What kind of gall did it take for her children to send their father running after her? And for him to actually do it?

Lacey slipped her phone out of her pocket, her thumb hovering above Maddie's face. Then she turned the phone face down on her bed. She shouldn't talk to her daughter with all this anger burning through her. She didn't want to be one of those moms who broke a relationship due to unkind words.

She turned her thoughts toward Sean. That relationship, she could break. Hell, he broke it decades ago when he moved back to Dallas and left her and the kids in California. And she didn't need him at all anymore. It had been years since he'd paid child support, and both kids had made it through college. She didn't understand why he thought he had any power over her at all. He might have flown halfway around the world to tell her how to spend her retirement, but she'd throw him overboard before she'd listen.

Finally secure in her plan, she marched to the viewing room. Sean had arrived first and lounged at a semicircular bench nestled around a small table. He gazed out at the sea and hadn't seen her, so Lacey went straight to the bar and ordered a vodka tonic, double.

She took a long sip of the icy drink before turning back to Sean. Just seeing him made her angry. She'd really cared about him once. Some sliver of that long ago love still existed in her heart. But he'd ruined it. And now he wanted to ruin her retirement, to chase her down and make her live out some dull existence as a regular person when she wanted to be free.

A sigh escaped her lips. She might as well get their conversation over with and get him off this boat.

Lacey placed the bakery bag on the small table, then slipped in beside him. "There are sandwiches in the bag, and if they're anywhere near as good as the pastries this morning, you'll love them. Help yourself."

"You've already ordered a drink? It's not even noon yet."

He'd barely gotten the words out of his mouth before she exploded. "Are you here to tell me when I can drink? Or worse, what I should do with my retirement? I'm a fucking grown ass woman. Do you remember me at all? The last thing in the world I need is someone telling me what to do. Particularly someone with your lousy track record." It surprised her that flames didn't erupt from her tongue as she spoke.

Sean lifted his hands, perhaps in surrender, perhaps to protect himself. "Lacey, I'm sorry. I started us off on the wrong foot and haven't been totally honest with you. The kids didn't ask me to check up on you. In fact, they don't even know I'm here." His sheepish look told the truth.

"What? Then why are you here?"

"When Zach told me you'd jaunted off on a cruise of the Norwegian coast, well, it sounded like the kind of thing I've always wanted to do. It's the kind of thing I should be doing. I can't remember the last time I took a big, exciting trip. I mean look at this, it's gorgeous." He waved his hand toward the expansive windows. The boat slid past a tiny green island topped by a quaint canary-colored house.

The peaceful view calmed her down a notch. "But you could have taken a trip anywhere. Why come bother me here?"

"Oh. Wow. I guess I didn't think I'd be a bother. I thought it would be fun. When I heard about this trip, it reminded me of being with you. You always had such a great spirit of adventure. I've never met anyone else who honeymooned in Chile, yet you convinced me that's where we should go."

"I thought you loved Chile." Their honeymoon had been the best trip of her life, one she treasured still.

Sean sat up straighter, his eyes shining with memory, and Lacey thought he almost reached for her hand. She drew hers back quickly.

"I did love Chile. It's the most exciting place I've ever been. Remember Señora Nalda's?"

How could she forget? They'd spent two days in bed at the guesthouse in the coastal town of Viña del Mar, barely leaving the room except when starved for food. They'd left their responsibilities thousands and thousands of miles away, and that freed them somehow. The sex had been wild, and amazing.

"I loved it too." She didn't know why her voice sounded forlorn. Maybe this trip and the cruise life would help her rediscover that uninhibited, more loving part of herself. She'd hardened over the years.

She stared at Sean, trying to see deep into him. He probably missed that part of himself as well. But couldn't he go on his own adventure instead of disturbing hers?

They sat in silence. Eventually, he pulled the bakery bag into his lap. "Turkey and ham. Can I have the ham?"

"Of course. I may not have any since I ate three pastries this morning."

"Now, see. That's what I love about you. The women I'm around count every calorie and have to tell you about it. You just kind of go with the flow."

"Yeah. I remember how I just went with the flow when you decided you needed to be in Dallas for your real estate career to flourish." She couldn't resist the jab.

Sean steepled his fingers, then dropped his head. Maybe she shouldn't have brought up the decades-old argument, but her first major betrayal still hurt. She no longer cried over this one the way she'd cried about the promotion rejection on her morning walk, but the first wound cut deepest.

Sean looked up and gazed directly into her eyes. "It was the right thing to do for my career, and the wrong thing to do for our family. You could have come with me. You didn't even try to look for a job in Dallas."

"But I had a good job, a great job. Why does the woman always have to be the one to give up?" Lacey had returned to her thirties, the hurt and indignation welling up as it had then.

"It wasn't about gender. You know I'm not like that. All the commercial real estate firms in San Diego were father-son teams. I never would have made partner in a firm like that."

"Stop. We've both got to stop. It doesn't matter anymore anyway. The kids are grown and they're doing great. In the end, that's all that matters." She didn't want to argue, at least not about this. "I need another drink. Can I get you something?"

"I'll get it." Sean looked at her and must have seen the raised eyebrows. "Please, let me buy you a drink. I've come in here and caused a big fuss. It's the least I can do. What are you drinking?"

"I think I'm going to switch to red wine. See if they have a cab or a chianti. Something full bodied. And thank you." She relaxed into her chair. He was on the ship until at least the next stop. She might as well catch up and see if he had any new info about the kids.

He came back with a bottle and two glasses. "They had a descent Rioja." He poured the ruby liquid into the stemware, then raised his toward her. "To your retirement."

"I'll drink to that." She raised her own glass and clinked it against his. This could have been a celebration of their retirement, had he stuck around. She pushed the unwelcome thought away. There was as much water under that bridge as in the sea around them.

"Is anything new going on with the kids?" She took a sip of the wine, which filled her mouth with fruit and vines and the taste of Spain.

"You mean other than their all-consuming attempt to save the world we destroyed? No, not much."

"I can't believe we raised such do-gooders. I always feel guilty around them," Lacey said.

"I know exactly what you mean. I thought Maddie would be proud of me for buying an electric truck, but she gave me a lecture on why I shouldn't replace my cars so often instead."

"Yep, I've heard that one. I'm going to drive my Prius until the wheels fall off. Have you gone vegetarian yet?"

"Are you kidding? You know I love a good steak. My not eating red meat can't be the only way to stop climate change." He took a long sip of wine. "Damn. That's good."

"It's delicious. I try not to eat meat or seafood in front of them, but I haven't made any promises. I do recycle."

"Everybody recycles."

Lacey sighed. "Why do I always feel so guilty about the world we left them?"

"Because it sucks. You should be glad you didn't move back to Texas with me. The politics are crazy. It's like no one is normal anymore. You either have to be a rabid right-wing nut job or a crying liberal."

"I'm liberal and I'm not crying."

He half-chuckled, then slumped back into his seat. "I'm just so tired. Tired of all of it. I work like a dog, but I don't really like the people I work with. Hell, there aren't many people I do like anymore, but god knows, they all think I love them. I don't want to talk politics. I don't want to hear about how America is ruined when I look around and see a great country that I love. People are nuts these days." He ran a hand through his hair, signaling his frustration by pulling at it the way he used to when they argued.

"Maybe you should retire. I highly recommend it."

This time he laughed, and she joined in. She got it. Before she retired, she'd always had to be careful about what she said. It had become so easy to offend someone, and incredibly easy to be offended by ridiculous politicians. But the kids bore the brunt of it, trying to do good in a time that seemed increasingly evil.

"It's fantastic to see you," Sean said. "It's been such a long time since I've been able to have an intelligent conversation with someone who really knows me."

"Do you not talk to Sheryl anymore?" Sean had married his second wife after moving back to Dallas. Lacey almost didn't bring her up since she hated the woman, but he seemed so lonely.

Sean snorted. "I talk to her about the boys, and only when necessary. Besides, she and I never had too many intellectually stimulating conversations."

"That's what you get for marrying the office bimbo with the big boobs. By the way, I hope you don't talk bad about me when I'm not around."

"Never." He winked at her, then grew serious. "I was such a dumbass when I was younger. I never should have left you. I mean, I wouldn't give up the two boys for anything, but I shouldn't have married Sheryl. Coming home to that woman became painful."

"Yeah. She's never been my favorite. Thanks for making it so I didn't have to talk to her much after that one incident." Lacey would never forget Sheryl calling her and asking her to forgo any future child support payments because they were too poor now that she and Sean had their own two kids. Lacey had said no immediately, furious that Sean would have gotten himself into a financial position that might endanger their children's future. Sheryl tried crying and yelling before Lacey finally hung up the phone.

She'd called Sean immediately. Halfway through chewing him out, he convinced her to stop and listen. He had no intention of stopping the child support payments, and he revealed that Sheryl's call stemmed from his refusing to buy her a new house, not from any financial difficulties. She heard his cold fury through the phone, and he asked her to hang up on Sheryl if she ever called again. Aside from polite greetings at graduations, Lacey hadn't spoken to the woman since.

"I think that may have been the maddest I've ever been in my life," Sean said. "I wanted to divorce her that very day. The marriage was already fraying, but I needed to stick something out for once in my life, so I waited until the boys left for college."

"I'm glad you did. Not to burden you with any more guilt, but I think it helps children to have a dad around."

"Touché."

They sat in silence, sipping their wine and watching coastal Norway pass outside the window. Their past settled between them, making the air heavier but somehow more comforting. She'd known Sean longer than almost any person she kept up with, and he'd always be an important part of her past. Her future too, perhaps, as the kids got older and married and had children.

"I think it's time to let go of the past, at least the bad parts of it. You tried to be a good dad." She tilted her glass toward him.

His eyebrows raised. She had surprised him. He clinked his glass against hers. "Here's to starting over."

"To retirement," she quipped, suddenly afraid he meant the two of them. "You should try it."

"Let's say this is my test drive." He nodded toward the window. "So far, so good."

"Uhm. This is my test drive." She could let her ancient anger at him slip away, but that didn't mean she wanted to be saddled with him for the rest of the trip.

"I thought maybe you'd like a co-pilot. And I really need to figure out my life. If I don't make a change soon, I'm going to die at my desk. I don't want to be like my dad, retiring in my late seventies when I'm finally kicked out of the office by my partners."

Sean's father had been an attorney who prided himself on two things, working every day except the sabbath and his Dallas Country Club membership. Lacey had heard Sean say he didn't want to be like his dad from the moment they'd met. And he wasn't. He had none of his father's coldness or judgement. But Sean did prioritize work, at least he always had. As had she.

"Do you think we both worked so hard because of the generation we grew up in?" she asked.

"I'm not sure. I certainly know plenty of slackers my age, but most of the people I still hang out with from our class are still pretty engaged in work. Most are successful. At least most of the men."

"Ain't that the truth." Lacey only kept up with one girlfriend from college. Probably half the women in her freshman dorm at SMU had announced their intention to get an MRS degree early on. She wondered how that had worked out for them.

"Do you think Maddie and Zach will work as hard as we did?" Sean asked.

"God, I hope not. Although they're so passionate about what they're doing, they'll probably end up outworking us." She worried about them finding balance in their lives, but she had never set a great example.

"Those two are definitely out to save the world. I feel pretty guilty about that sometimes. We left them with a real shit show," Sean said.

"Oh, my god. I feel exactly the same. I always thought we were doing the right thing. Then my life flashes by and everything I thought was right ends up being wrong. Trickle-down economics, capitalism. Hell, I thought I'd saved the world by buying an Earth Day T-shirt. It was all bullshit."

"There's the Lacey I know, getting all fired up about things. You know, the kids got that from you."

"Yeah, but they're saving the world. We're the ones who wrecked it."

"Well, I like to put most of that blame on the folks older than us. Lower taxes, busting unions, those were their ideas." Sean refilled their wineglasses.

"Yeah, but we just followed along like blind puppies. Most of those guys are still in control. Have you looked at who's leading our government and corporations? Hell, half of the rock bands from the seventies are still touring." Lacey twirled the garnet liquid, then held it up to the grass green hills beyond the window.

Sean sighed deeply. "You know, when I told Zach I was thinking about retiring, he suggested I move to San Francisco and start volunteering. He told me he could hook me up with the right people." Sean shook his head, seeming to mirror her feelings about how mixed up the world had become.

"Same. That's part of the reason I had to get away. I've worked so hard. I earned this retirement. I felt like I had to escape." Something warm lit in her chest. He understood her. They shared the same situation.

"You did earn your retirement." He patted her knee, then took out a sandwich and started eating.

Lacey relaxed, feeling the alcohol swirl through her veins. That, plus the gentle movement of the boat calmed her. It was like being back in the womb, safe and protected, with someone else responsible for your direction. Her eyes closed. It had been an early morning.

"Hey, Lacey." Sean spoke softly, as if he feared she'd fallen asleep. "Do you ever worry about being bored in retirement?"

Her eyelids flung open. She hadn't considered that, not really. But perhaps she'd kept herself busy these past weeks so she wouldn't have to think about things like that.

"I can't imagine it." Of course not. That's why she'd chosen the cruise. It would keep her occupied unless she chose to stop and relax. She shuddered thinking about the tiny condo she'd bought. Staying there every day with nothing to do except watch the people around her age sounded like torture. She'd bought that as insurance, just in case whatever she ended up doing next didn't work out. For now, she had to keep moving.

"I worry about that a little. I like the idea of travel, although I need a place to come home to." He looked a little sad, perhaps because he hadn't figured it out yet. Lacey had. She'd travel and have fun, but she had the condo if she needed it. Sean was different.

"Yes, you always wanted to go home." She couldn't help the biting comment. She'd said she'd forgive him and move on, but falling back into her old habit of striking out at the things he'd done wrong was too easy. "Sorry."

"Nope, I deserve it. Speaking of being bored, have you signed up for any of the excursions? Some of them look amazing."

"I'm going on the silent whale cruise tomorrow. The kids would love it, because the tour boat is a hybrid. There's no engine noise to bother the whales." She couldn't wait for the excursion and prayed they spotted the animals.

"Do you mind if I tag along?" He wore that hopeful look again. Something about it reminded her of the younger Sean, the one she'd known before all their trouble.

"Sure. But you better sign up. They only have so many openings."

He stood. "Can I take you to dinner tonight—at the nice restaurant on board?"

This yes seemed a little more dangerous. But she was tired of spending time with Alexander and Marie, and she had been wanting to try the upscale eatery.

"Sure." She returned his smile, hoping he didn't get the wrong idea.

Chapter 9

Lacey woke from her nap with a red wine headache and cottonmouth. In a strange way, it cemented her retirement. It eerily reminded her of college days, when waking with a hangover happened far more often than in the following decades.

She needed to take stock of this new life. Nothing would change the fact that Sean had joined her cruise, but she had to claim this life and make it her own. Having a drink or two and talking to an old friend in the middle of the day could be an occasional part of her retirement plan. In fact, she should reach out to friends on her various journeys and see if anyone wanted to join her.

But she also needed more structure. For decades, she'd been a woman with planned days. She worked long hours during the week, leaving the relatively few weekend hours for the remaining things life required: grocery shopping, gardening, occasionally replacing a suit or pair of shoes at the mall. And of course she left time for fun.

But now, long days stretched in front of her, and she needed a plan. She'd heard you should drink a gallon of water a day. Maybe she could do that every day. Although she'd have to pee every five minutes. She grabbed a notebook and wrote *drink more water.*

Given her recent meals of pastries and a carb and meat heavy breakfast buffet, she needed to mix in a few vegetables. Every day. She could relive some of the fun of youth while recognizing her older body demanded more care.

She pulled a pair of black yoga pants out of a drawer. Exercise. Every day. Starting today. Surely the daily water, veg, and workout plan would keep her healthy. She rarely fell sick and didn't know of any worrisome genetic issues. She might not get to choose the quantity of life she had left, but she sure wanted optimal quality. If she played it right, she'd remain healthy until the day she dropped dead. So wine was fine, and keeping up her health, divine.

Lacey shook her head as she closed the cabin door. What, now she was a poet? She made her way to the deck and began striding around the boat. The cool air invigorated her. How wonderful that her daily exercise included an ocean view. The workout machines in the weight room had a similar view. Maybe she could find a class or two to attend. This boat didn't offer any, but her research showed that other ships did. She'd attended Jazzercize classes for decades and loved anything with a good beat and steps to learn. Zumba had been her favorite. Sunday afternoons she'd reserved for a yoga stretch class at the Y. Maybe she could recreate most of it in her cramped cabin.

Every time her mind wandered toward dinner with Sean, she refocused on getting her new life in order. She could set a monthly to-do list as well. In Carlsbad, she'd had one that would be easy to recreate here. She could focus on retirement self-care. Regardless of her location, the first week of the month she'd get a facial, the second a massage, and the third a mani-pedi. The final week she reserved for her haircut. Any onboard salon would accommodate all of these. Time to open her calendar and make some appointments.

With her new life now arranged, she had nothing left to plan and five more laps of the deck before she finished her workout. Of course dinner with Sean overtook her thoughts.

No romantic feelings, just friends. He'd been the only guy she'd truly loved. Long ago, she thought she loved her high school boyfriend, but Sean had shown her the difference between puppy love and the real thing. Although at seventeen, she couldn't imagine a life without Curt. Oh, the passion of youth. The remembered longing for that boy sent a jolt of electricity through her.

They'd started dating at sixteen, and on her seventeenth birthday she'd lost her virginity. After that, they'd basically become sex monkeys, searching for any moment either of their parents left home for a few hours, not to mention the blanket he kept in the back of his pickup for dusty back roads.

She swore when she left for college, they'd stay together forever. Like most couples of that age, it didn't work out. Sometime freshman year they'd mutually called it quits and moved on. He'd stayed in El Paso for college and lived there still with his wife and four kids. Lacey moved to Dallas and jumped into an exciting world where she saw new things, met new people, and pressed herself toward success.

Which eventually led her to Sean in her organizational behavior class junior year. And here he was so many years later, bouncing into her life unexpectedly, and unexpectedly single. And she hadn't been laid in years.

STOP.

She could hang out with him for a few days while she developed her sea legs and learned how to negotiate being alone on a ship full of couples. She'd enjoyed talking to him, just the way she would have enjoyed speaking with anyone who shared her past. That was all.

She puffed around the deck one last time. Her new plan put her life in order. Sean had caused a small quake in this first cruise, but she would overcome this, learn from it. As long as she controlled her actions, everything would be fine.

Lacey swept the Dior stick across her lips. The berry color added a brightness to her face that she needed now that she'd gone gray. Hopefully, Sean wouldn't notice she'd spent thirty minutes in front of the mirror doing her makeup and hair and retying her scarf to the side, which left her cleavage on show. Not that she was trying to seduce him, she just wanted to look good. And she did, for her age.

She loved the platinum hair that she'd quit dyeing during COVID. Instead of making her look older, something about it made her blue eyes sparkle more than before, but a little lipstick still helped. Her skin glowed, thanks to regular facials and good makeup, but she'd gained more than a few lines along the way.

Thanks to her dance classes, she appreciated the strength of her body, and the yoga had kept her naturally stretchy. She tried to fan the heat off her face. Sean had been the first one to call her stretchy, and it had nothing to do with yoga. At sixty, she wasn't that kind of stretchy anymore. Besides, that's not what any of this was about.

She had to stop creating drama that didn't exist. Still, as she walked toward the restaurant, something harder than butterflies knocked around her stomach. Despite how many times she'd told herself dinner meant nothing, his flying all the way to Norway to meet her on a ship had to mean something.

The elevator doors slid open, and she caught sight of him standing near the restaurant entrance. She almost let the doors close without stepping out. Sean had always looked good in a suit. The silver mixed in with dark brown at his temples gave him a distinguished air he'd lacked in his frat boy youth. He also seemed slimmer, fitter, than he had back then. Not that she should think about his body.

What the hell was wrong with her? She hated acting like a schoolgirl with a crush. This man had almost single-handedly destroyed her life. He'd left her with two small kids and retreated to Dallas, where he thought making money would be easier. She'd hated that leaving was the easy path for him. He'd rejected not only her but their children, forcing them into uncomfortable vacations and summers spent in the sweltering Dallas heat instead of on the beaches of Southern California. The kids eventually put a stop to that, partly because they wanted to attend summer camps with their friends, partly because of the new wife's coldness once she had her own brood.

That remnant of anger took care of any lingering thoughts of desire, and Lacey strode out to meet him. For some reason, her hand came out as if to shake his. He looked at it with a curious expression, then used it to draw her into a hug.

Discombobulated, she wrapped an arm around him, then quickly pulled back. Best not to fall into an embrace of strong arms.

The waiter led them to a corner table and presented the menus. Lacey threw her shoulders back, feeling sophisticated in her deep teal silk dress. The elegant, understated surroundings had minimalist blond wood and white tablecloths. She sank into the emerald suede high back chair. Despite the hefty chair, she teetered as if off balance. Should she be here? Worse, why did dinner with her ex cause these strange feelings?

She took a deep breath and tried to center herself. While she hadn't expected this, she'd spent half her work life putting out fires. She could deal with it. She would recover, pivot, all those things she'd made others do over the years.

She accepted the menu from the waiter and perused the selection of appetizers. A loud guffaw escaped, despite her trying to stifle it. "Should we start with the truffled seaweed?"

"Actually, I think I'll start with the pumpkin puree and sea urchin," Sean said, deadpan.

Lacey tried to keep a straight face but couldn't match his demeanor. She glanced at the next appetizer on the list. "Oh, but we wouldn't want to miss the burnt cabbage and seaweed soup topped with caviar."

"You always did make life interesting." Laugh lines creased the corners of his eyes, and though he attempted to suppress a full smile, his mouth tweaked up in a grin.

"Oh, no," Lacey said after she read the next appetizer which featured moose bone marrow. "Maddie would hate that they serve moose. In fact, I don't want to eat something that cute."

"That's nothing. They've got reindeer steak as a main course. She might have heart failure if her parents ate that."

"I may have to go vegetarian tonight, in her honor. Do they have anything suitable?" Maddie went vegetarian at twelve. A few years later, she convinced her brother to do the same. Lacey had become an expert at fixing healthy vegetable-based meals, although she still snuck the occasional hamburger or sushi at work lunches. She didn't share her cheats with her kids, and they likely thought she didn't eat meat.

"They've got the perfect vegetarian alternative,' Sean said. "Baked celery with fried yeast." His face grew red, and a chortle escaped.

Lacey couldn't take it anymore. Laughter burst from her. The crazy dishes were exactly what she wanted out of life on the sea. Something strange and new and different from the staid life she'd lived while chained to a desk all those years. How lucky that she got to share this moment with someone else from Texas who would find the offerings as bizarre as she did. Pure joy accompanied the humor.

"I'm going to have that damn celery, and I bet it will be the best thing I've ever eaten."

"Yeah, I'm going to stick with the arctic char. Just don't tell the kids."

"Do you pretend to be a vegetarian when they're around too?"

"Hell no. I'm always taking them to the steakhouse and trying to get them to eat meat."

"That's cruel. Why would you do that to your children?" She giggled, the comment far more funny than cruel. The kids had no trouble sticking up for themselves.

"Yeah, well, I figured with all the money they've convinced me to donate to environmental organizations over the years, they owed me at least a burger. And it turns out they were right after all."

Lacey wanted to ask him what he meant, but the waiter stopped by to take their order. He even accommodated her request for a vegetarian appetizer. Sean ordered a bottle of champagne. Lacey raised her brows at that, but he just gave her a wink.

"Let's celebrate raising two great kids and your retirement." A heartfelt smile lit his face.

"Sure. Hey, what did you mean when you said it turns out they were right after all?"

He sighed heavily. "I've had a little heart trouble over the past year. I'm all patched up with a couple of stents, but red meat is definitely off the table. I should have listened to the kids. At least that's what Zach said when I told them."

"I'm so sorry to hear about that. I'm surprised they didn't tell me." Talk about having to face mortality.

"I asked them not to. We didn't need to bother you about it and everything turned out fine." He ran a hand through his hair, rumpling it. The motion swept the years away. She'd always preferred the rumpled look. "I think, maybe, that's part of the reason I came out here and surprised you. I need to figure out what to do with the years I have left. I want them to be more meaningful than the ones that went before."

His dark eyes stared into hers, eyes she used to get lost in. But they'd aged along with the rest of him, lids sagging a little, fine lines in his face that added gravitas. They both had far fewer years in front of them than behind them. His health issue scared her.

"Are you sure you're going to be okay?"

"I'm fine. Better than before, except I'm still on too many medications. But as long as I stay healthy, exercise, cut out the bad foods I love, I'll live a long time yet."

The waiter returned with their champagne. She loved its apricot color and the way the bubbles caught the light as they rose to the surface.

"To your retirement." Sean tipped his glass toward her.

"To your health." She met his glass with the lightest of clinks.

The delicate wine tickled her mouth, and flavors of rose, mineral, and honey greeted her tongue. "That's wonderful."

"So are you. Thanks for all you did with the kids. They're fantastic. The other two boys are knuckleheads compared to Maddie and Zach."

"Don't say that. They're your kids." Still, she'd heard about their middling grades and wrecked cars.

"They'll be fine when they're older, but they'll never have the same passion about the world as our two."

As the conversation progressed, Lacey's wall of tension crumbled brick by brick. In its place, she forged a new relationship with her ex. She'd forgotten how charming he could be, and how funny. They'd rarely had time for jokes when discussing the kids, their sole subject of conversation, post-divorce.

By the time they'd made it through dessert, local cloudberries with white chocolate cream, her cheeks burned from smiling. The night had been one of her most enjoyable in years.

They said goodbye just outside the restaurant doors. She wanted to wander the ship for a while before returning to her cabin.

"Thank you for dinner. You didn't have to pay," she said. He didn't have to pick up the hefty tab. But it meant something that he had.

"I wanted to. It's fantastic to catch up with you."

He paused for a moment. Lacey wondered if he wanted to lean in and kiss her. She tried to jerk the unwelcome thought from her brain. Been there, done that.

"Well, thanks again. I'll probably see you tomorrow." She turned and hurried toward the library doors. She didn't want to ruin a good evening with questions about what might be next.

Chapter 10

Lacey had signed up for the silent whale watching tour on the first day of the cruise. She couldn't wait to tell Maddie about it and share photos with her. Her daughter would love the environmentally friendly electric boats used for the tour. They emitted no air or sound pollution.

She had to be off the cruise ship before sunrise and wore almost every piece of warm clothing she'd brought: long underwear, two pairs of socks, a sweater, a fleece jacket, and a down jacket on top of that. She even wore a wool beanie and down mittens she'd purchased in the ship's boutique.

Even so, when she stepped off the ship, the cold bit into her, making her eyes instantly tear. She waddled down the ramp in her snow-man attire to where Sean waited below.

"Is everything okay?" he asked.

She wiped the tears plunging down her face with a mittened hand. "Yes, the cold makes my eyes water—one of the side effects of getting old."

Just then, the group leader, complete with a huge sign bearing the name of their boat, asked them to get in line and follow him. Walking in pairs behind their leader reminded her of a kindergarten class following the teacher. This certainly wasn't up close and personal tourism. In college, she and a friend had used Eurail passes to tromp around southern Europe. Cruise travel didn't offer that kind of freedom. Although she wasn't twenty anymore either.

Their short walk led to a multistory catamaran with open viewing decks and a tall center section with glass windows. It relieved her to see plenty of room inside and out of the elements. Another sign of being old.

Lacey and Sean bought cups of coffee and pastries and took seats near the windows at the highest level of the boat. Diesel engines started, then the vessel left its mooring.

"I thought this was supposed to be an electric boat." Her comment came out louder than expected, but she'd looked forward to an environmentally friendly outing.

Lacey's comment caught the attention of a woman with long dark hair staring out the windows. She turned and approached.

"Hello, I'm Valerie, the marine biologist leading this tour. I overheard your question about the engines." The woman's warm brown eyes relieved any embarrassment over being caught questioning the tour.

"Thanks. I was just surprised when I heard the engines start. I thought the boat was electric."

"We will use the electric engines once we are nearer the whales because the sound bothers them. However, we have a long way to go to reach the feeding grounds. For that, we use the diesel engines."

"You're not Norwegian, are you?" Sean asked. No doubt he'd caught her delightful accent, not to mention the dark coloring.

"No, I am from Italy. I came here for my Ph.D. research."

"No fish left in Italy?"

Lacey hated Sean's comment. He was trying to impress the woman with humor, and Lacey had seen that maneuver before. Why couldn't guys just talk to women like normal people?

"I'm studying the effects of climate change on the oceans, and they are really just one big system. What happens in one area affects all others. For migrating species like whales and the herring they feed on, warmer ocean temperatures are changing ancient migration patterns."

"Our kids would love you. One is an environmental attorney and the other an activist." Lacey couldn't help lumping Valerie into the new generation of young people fighting to save the planet, even though she was a few years older than Maddie.

"It is good to hear of people from the United States doing this kind of work. I wish your government were more serious about climate change."

"I wish they were more serious, period." The words slipped out before Lacey could stop them. The US had such a clown show of national politicians that it embarrassed her in international conversations.

"In thirty minutes, I'll be giving a briefing on what species we're likely to see today. It will be just over there if you'd like to join me." She pointed to an area with a podium and a projector screen.

"We'll be there." Lacey and Sean spoke simultaneously. It made her giggle. The woman had to think they were married since she'd mentioned the kids, and now they had synchronous thoughts. If only she knew.

Valerie left, and Lacey turned back toward the window. The sun crested the horizon as a glowing yellow ball in a pale blue sky. Every day in Norway had been cloudy, but this morning, not a single white puff graced the heavens. It must be an omen that good things would happen.

"Honey, I saw whales yesterday. Live ones swimming in the open ocean." Lacey had been too tired to call Maddie when she got back from the tour, but she picked up the phone early the next morning to reach her daughter before she went to bed. "It was incredible, and it made me so proud of what you do."

"Mom, I work for a land trust. We don't have anything to do with whales."

"I know, but you're trying to save the world. The marine biologist on the boat taught us so much about how climate change affects everything in the ocean, from corals to currents. I know you've talked to me about climate change for years, and of course I believe in it, but the thought of losing such magnificent creatures kills me." Lacey's connection to the world had deepened at the sight of the orca pod. Learning how social they were, how they worked as a team to accomplish their goals, and how females led the group, it gave some ancient, witchy meaning to how she'd spent her own life.

"I'm glad you learned that. Everything is connected. Right now, we're trying to find enough land to protect honeybees. If you want to talk connected, try eating a meal a bee didn't play a role in."

Lacey tried to detect any snark or accusation in her daughter's comment. If it existed, Lacey deserved it. She could see now that she'd talked the environmental talk but had let her kids do the walking. But Maddie sounded, if anything, exhausted.

"Honey, are you okay?"

"I'm fine. It's just been a long day at work. Sometimes I feel like we lose more battles than we win. We're outmanned, outgunned. It's not a fair fight."

Lacey could picture the furrow between Maddie's eyebrows, could almost hear her worrying her hands. She wished she could heal this hurt with a hug and a kiss, the way she easily took care of younger wounds. But climate change heralded a global war, not a playground injury.

"I wish I could help." Empty words.

"Thanks, Mom. You could if you really wanted to. I've offered you a place to stay."

"Well, I'll be going into Deb's mom's place soon, but I could come up for Thanksgiving. I'd be happy to cook, or to take people out to dinner."

"Yeah, maybe. I'm not sure what Dad's plans are."

Heat surged through Lacey. They hadn't told the kids they'd met up on the cruise, and she hated the deception. But answering questions about their relationship had its own difficulties.

"Speaking of Dad, I've got a weird question for you. When he didn't answer his texts yesterday, I tried calling the office. His secretary said he was in Norway also. You haven't seen him, have you?"

Oh, god. She couldn't outright lie to her daughter. But what would she say? She and Sean hadn't discussed it yet.

"Mom?"

Lacey had waited too long. "Well, Norway is a big country." She knew the line would give her away the moment she uttered it, not to mention the cracking voice.

"Unbelievable. Why didn't you tell me?" Lacey could hear the little girl hurt in Maddie's voice. She recalled the many times over the years that her daughter had asked why she and Sean couldn't stay together. That question had been like a knife plunging into her each time, and even though she wanted to answer *because Daddy's a dickhead*, she never did. Not once.

"Honey, it was a surprise to me too. He just showed up. I guess Zach told him where I was. I'd been walking around Trondheim, and when I got back to the boat, there he was." Lacey took a deep breath and reclaimed her honesty.

"And?"

"And nothing. We're hanging out some, but we're not together or anything. Just friends."

"That seems weird."

It did seem weird. But also, it seemed like the most natural thing in the world.

"I'm sorry, but the kids know you're here." Lacey had found Sean in their favorite nook in the viewing room. They met there midmornings and read or talked until lunchtime. "Maddie talked to your secretary and then ambushed me by asking if I knew you were in Norway, and I just can't lie to that girl. She always knows."

"Huh."

She'd expected surprise or worry, but he seemed unruffled. "I thought you'd be traumatized by the information. I sure am."

"The one thing I don't have to worry about with you is whether the kids approve. They think you walk on water, especially compared to my track record with women."

"Huh." She hadn't looked at it that way before. She had heard little about his life after he divorced Sheryl. Maybe he'd had women show up at holidays when the kids went to Dallas.

She opened her book, a thriller by a well-known author. It had been years since she'd read as much as she had lately. She loved that retirement perk but wished she still had her Kindle instead of confining her reading to what the library had on offer.

She sighed, starting the page anew after her mind wandered. She just couldn't get into this one. Maybe she'd read it before and just didn't remember.

She glanced at Sean's book. The history of the Premier League. She recognized David Beckham on the cover, more because of his glamorous lifestyle than any adoration for soccer.

"I think I'm going to visit the library and pick out a different book," she said.

He looked up, then slid her book out of her hands. He turned it over and read the back cover. "I'll take this one if you'll take mine back."

"Sure. I wondered about your sudden interest in soccer."

"All this reading is going to lead me to start day drinking. I miss TV."

Lacey chuckled. "We've already been day drinking. Almost every day."

She returned the soccer book to the library and started searching for something new. His comment made some sense. She'd hardly thought about TV since she'd been onboard, but it used to be a far larger part of her life. It was so easy to come home and let someone else's words and ideas flow over her after a day of difficult personal interactions, deadlines, and ridiculous bosses. TV's passive entertainment let her quit thinking and lose herself in someone else's creativity.

Reading seemed much more active. A book combined the author's words with her imagination to create something unique.

She perused the shelves, looking for the perfect book to draw her into its world. A bright cover caught her eye, and she picked up the novel—a mystery set in the Midwest where everything happened in and around a Filipino bakery. It sounded delicious.

When she opened it, she discovered the author had signed it. *To Marguerite, May love guide you to adventure. Mia.*

Well, she wasn't Marguerite, but love and adventure sounded right up her alley. Lacey closed the book and tucked it under her arm, certain it would be better than the latest show on Netflix.

By the time she got back to the viewing room, Sean had ordered a Scotch. She snuck to the bar before sitting down and asked for the same. When she reached their table, he had put his book aside and stared at her, drink in hand.

"Hey, it looks like you got a two-fer," he said, focused on her drink.

"I didn't want you to get too far ahead of me." She looked out across slate gray water. Last night had brought a dusting of snow that reached almost to the water's edge. This country was gorgeous. Sometimes she thought she might be able to sit forever on this very boat, traveling up and down the coast as the seasons changed. Instead, she had a whole globe's worth of coastline to explore.

"You know," said Sean. "I don't think I'm ready for this retirement thing. I'd get bored just reading all the time."

"And drinking," she added.

"Yeah, I could see that turning into an actual problem. There's just not enough to do."

Lacey sat with his words. Her exhaustion over decades of busting her butt left her wanting nothing more than to relax, luxuriate really, in the time that remained.

Certainly, she'd have to keep supplied with good books. And she had her daily schedule to keep her company. She could learn about the places she'd visit, meet new people. It still sounded like one big adventure, like in the book's inscription. Although there was no mention of love.

She thought about telling Sean that he'd always put his work first. But she didn't. Over the last few days, she'd grown to like him much more than she had in decades, and her ready comment sounded petty and mean.

"Well, then I guess it's a good thing we've got another tour tomorrow." They'd signed up for a bus ride on the Atlantic Road, a curvy island to island hop through the countryside. The trip left in the afternoon and would make a dinner stop. It wasn't the most active of tours, but the scenery looked spectacular.

"I'm looking forward to that. Thanks for letting me tag along. It's fun to be with you."

"It's fun to be with you too, and I have to admit, that's a little bit of a surprise." She took a sip of her drink so she'd stop talking. He looked as surprised at the words as she felt, but she'd spoken the truth. Her once-husband had become the companion she didn't know she wanted on this journey.

When he'd first shown up at her boat, she'd feared he'd arrived for her, somehow wanting to restart the relationship of the past. She wanted to look forward, move forward, not back.

But he hadn't come for her. He'd come for himself. She recognized the taking stock and trying to figure out what to do with what little of life remained. She predicted he'd end up back in Dallas, most likely dating women far too young. Until then, he could be her buddy on this trip.

Chapter 11

The next day the bus whizzed them down a two-lane road. They passed small towns, lakes, and miles of green fields. The entire time, Sean's thigh rested along Lacey's. He'd given her the window seat like a gentleman, but with such spectacular scenery, he'd leaned into her almost the entire trip.

Lacey loved it. The cold air emanating from the window met the heat coming off his body, and she basked in the middle. She had the perfect balance of brisk and toasty, like when her face stuck out of the covers on a cold winter's night, but the rest of her snuggled under heated blankets. She may have promised herself they'd just be friends, but her body clearly enjoyed the hip-to-hip warmth.

They'd already seen several ornate wooden churches that looked like elves had carved them centuries earlier. Now the bus meandered from island to island over windy roads and bridges. Some of the so-called islands barely made it past medium boulder size.

She'd entered another dimension in this cool, green, watery world. She struggled to believe that the plains of Texas or wide sand beaches of Southern California existed on the same planet as this. And she wasn't sure she wanted them to.

Over the past few days, she'd changed. The constant stress of work that had attached itself to her like a bad headache had disappeared. The frenzy of trying to figure out what to do next, of selling her house—how had she packed up an entire life and shoved it into storage in only thirty days—that frenzy had abandoned her as well. As she'd adjusted to the time change and the food on the other side of the world, time had slowed. The limited choices of life at sea had stripped her down to her core.

New sights, sounds, and tastes filled her with wonder. The ever-changing view out the window in the long days of a late Norwegian summer felt like discovering the world for the first time. She'd even found a new relationship in the old friend beside her.

Lacey marveled at how much had changed, how much she'd changed. Some crusty exterior, built over years of fending for herself at work and at home, had washed away here. It felt like starting over.

The bus pulled into a parking lot, and the passengers dutifully trudged around an island on a wooden boardwalk. Lacey felt like running ahead of the pack, frolicking like a foal in a field. She grabbed Sean's hand and pulled him forward.

The boardwalk curved around the base of a stone island. An enormous rock rose to their left, and calm waters splayed to their right. The world was a study in gray: soot-bottomed clouds threatened rain, graphite stone with charcoal flecks rose beside them, and silver water stretched into the distance. Yet all the gray made the colors brighter. The Kelly grass on a far shore, orange and yellow lichen clinging to stone, and the sheen of her burgundy puffy jacket burst from the somber day.

They turned a corner and spied an off-kilter bridge lifting steeply off the island toward the sky, then turning sharply and disappearing into nothing. She'd fallen into an Escher drawing where nothing quite made sense. She wanted to wrap her arms around this ridiculous world and never let go. She'd come home, not to Norway, but to herself.

Next, they stopped at a two-story restaurant built of sunflower-colored wood with a sod roof covered by bright green grass. The thirty or so people from the cruise filed in and sat at two long tables.

Baskets of bread topped the tables, and Lacey found herself ravenous. She spread a thick slice of crusty bread with a generous portion of butter. Sean ordered a beer and asked if she'd like one.

"No thanks." It sounded wonderful, but she didn't trust her sixty-year-old bladder to make the journey back full of beer.

Soon, steaming bowls of bacalao, Norwegian salt cod, were set down in front of the hungry patrons. Lacey wouldn't have ordered the stew off a menu, but it tasted like perfection. Warm and salty, the broth contained lots of vegetables and hunks of fish. They learned from the driver that dried fish had been a staple since Viking times, but visiting Spanish sailors originally created this particular dish hundreds of years earlier.

"We should have brought Maddie and Zach on this trip. They even have a vegetarian version of the soup." Lacey imagined traveling as an odd, grown-up family.

"How long have you been married?" asked the woman next to Sean. Lacey had often seen the woman and her elderly mother on the ship's deck.

"We were married almost thirty years ago." Sean jumped in before Lacey had a chance to say anything. He didn't mention that they'd been divorced more than half those years.

Lacey kicked him under the table and got a wink in return. Oh well, it's not like this friendly woman needed to hear her sob story.

"You two make a lovely couple," the woman said. "Mom was married for over fifty years before dad passed."

"I'm sorry to hear about your husband," Lacey said, turning to the woman beside her, who nodded back.

Lacey stifled the urge to tell the truth about her marriage. Now it would just be awkward. "Are you American?" Lacey asked.

"We're from San Francisco. I'm Krista, and this is my mother, Olga. You're from the states also?"

"Our kids are in San Francisco!" Lacey said with an abundance of emotion. "They both stayed up there after college."

The conversation continued with Lacey and Sean talking about the kids without ever needing to reveal their status. The mom never said a word, but Lacey hit it off with Krista, who'd been a financial controller at a tech company.

"Are you still working?" Lacey asked. The woman looked at least five years older than her.

"No, I retired years ago, although it sometimes feels like I still have a job with all the volunteer work I do. Thus, the vacation."

"Really? I just retired a month ago. This is my first time without a job since my freshman year of college. I can't tell you how much I'm enjoying this trip. Just today, on the bus, I felt like the real me had a chance to come out."

"Ah, the heady days of the newly retired. It took me a year to recover from working, but eventually I got bored."

"That's what I've been saying." Sean jumped into the conversation. "I don't know if I could travel full time. I've only been on board a short time and already I don't know what to do with myself."

"You'll figure it out. Some people take up hobbies, but I figured I might as well put my knowledge and experience to good use. It keeps me active and the organizations I help save money, which gives them the resources they need to go do good in the world."

Her words rankled Lacey, scratching against that belief that she'd done her share, and now she got to enjoy the spoils of her hard work. She didn't want to argue with Krista, who seemed perfectly happy. Perhaps different people needed different things in life. Also, Krista had her mother. Lacey's parents had passed years ago. Maybe she'd feel different if she had to take care of someone else.

Just then, the server swooped in and replaced their empty soup bowls with a crumbly cake with a bright yellow topping. He asked if they'd like coffee or a shot of aquavit. Sean said yes to both, as did Krista. She even ordered both for her mother.

"Me too," Lacey said, not wanting to be left out despite disliking the fiery Norwegian alcohol. Why not give it a second chance?

She tried the cake, and it tasted like a spongy granola bar topped with custard. The combined flavors of almonds, custard, and coffee were surprisingly delicious.

When they brought the aquavit, the old woman beside her raised the small glass in salute, drank the entire thing in one sip, and delicately placed the glass back on the table. Her fortitude amazed Lacey, and she followed with her own glass.

The burn in her throat brought tears to her eyes, but she liked it slightly better than the first time. Sean started coughing after drinking his.

"It's an acquired taste," said Krista.

"I guess," he said. "That'll sure clean the pipes."

They piled back on the bus, everyone seeming a little happier now that they'd had sustenance and drink. For Lacey, the burn of the liquor had settled into a warm glow that spread throughout her body.

After just a few miles, the bus turned onto a dirt road. They drove through stubby golden fields decorated with huge bales of straw. Twilight had arrived. On the ship, the evenings had seemed cozy as they glided past silent mountains or twinkling towns. Now, the cold coming in off the windows made the coming dark seem a more dangerous thing.

They arrived at a lake, or perhaps an inlet of sea, with a wide pebble beach. When she stepped off the bus, she saw a pyramid of wood.

"Come around for the bonfire." The tour leader gestured them forward. "For hundreds of years, since the time of the Vikings, we have built bonfires. They were used to signal danger, and to celebrate, usually on midsummer night. We are past midsummer today, but we wanted you to experience our bonfire."

"I hope they get that thing lit soon, it's freezing out here." Lacey rubbed her hands against her arms.

"Come here. I'll keep you warm." Sean wrapped an arm around her. She snuggled into him, ostensibly because of the cold, but also, he felt great. Maybe it was the aquavit or not having someone hold her in so long. Maybe it was because he'd been so damn nice this trip.

The fire built to a blaze quicker than Lacey expected. Soon the flames licked upward toward the sky, and the heat warmed her face.

The guide set up a table with hot chocolate and more aquavit. She grabbed one of each and took her firewater with a cocoa chaser. The drinks remedied the cold, but she snuggled into Sean anyway. Even after her body heat caused her to partially unzip her jacket.

"You know, we can just back away a little bit. We don't have to roast ourselves next to the fire."

Great idea. Lacey looked up at him and smiled, catching even more warmth from his gaze. She grabbed his hand and pulled him along the beach.

They looked out at the water, glowing red and yellow from the very last rays of the sun and the fire behind them. "It is so beautiful here," she said.

Sean turned her toward him. "What I'm looking at is beautiful."

Her breath caught. Then she shook her head. "You've been with far younger, far more beautiful women than me."

"Oh, Lacey." He almost growled the words. "Don't you know you've always been the one who got away?"

"But you had me. I wasn't the one who left."

"No. You weren't. I was definitely the asshole. Although, by the time I did go, I think you were ready."

She didn't say anything, but his comment rang true. She'd been so mad at him for wanting to take away her future, the kids' future, in the wonderful Mayberry they'd fallen into. Forgiving him had been impossible then, but she was someone different now.

"We both made mistakes," she said.

"Losing you was my worst mistake."

Lacey caught the glint of a tear sliding down his cheek, and her own eyes filled. "I'm so sorry we didn't try harder to work it out."

His hand reached gently to her jaw, then cradled her head. Slowly, he pulled her toward him and lowered his head until their lips met. Sparks and flames bigger than a bonfire lit her body, just the way they had the first time she'd kissed him junior year.

"Oh, my god, I'd forgotten what that was like." He'd barely pulled away to whisper the words.

She reached up and pulled him back to her lips. She wrapped her arms around his neck, and he followed and pulled her close. Pressing her body against his, she wished the layers of down between them would disappear. She wanted to feel his skin, melt into him the way she used to. She wanted to be loved.

A hunger opened as they kissed. Hell, this wasn't kissing, they were full on making out like the bonfire had transported her to the wild deserts of El Paso and the bonfires at high school keg parties. She'd made out there a time or two, but never like this. Never with such need and such certainty about where they'd end up tonight. She shivered just thinking about it.

"Are you getting cold again?" Sean asked.

"Not a chance," she whispered back.

Too soon, they heard the tour guide calling everyone to get back on the bus. He had little success. As people milled around the dying flames. Lacey and Sean walked back, hand-in-hand, and she wished they could climb aboard the ship instead of a bus with who knows how far to go before it dropped them off.

Almost unbelievably, the bus pulled beside the ship ten minutes later. The entire time, Sean draped himself over her and nibbled on her ear. She had a hand on his thigh and fantasized about moving it higher.

She stumbled on the ramp up to the boat, but Sean had an arm around her and kept her from falling. Sure, she'd had a lot to drink, but she could feel that haziness fading. She didn't want to think about mistakes or repercussions. She didn't want to worry about the future. She wanted sex.

They waited for their turn on the elevator. Once on board, Lacey grabbed his hand. She pressed in close to him so more people could fit.

"Would you like to go get a nightcap?" Sean whispered, his lips just an inch from her ear.

She turned to look at him. "No, I'm good." Then she squeezed his hand.

When they reached her floor, she pulled him off the elevator. He didn't resist.

It was all she could do to not disrobe as they made their way down the hallway. At last, they reached her door. She turned, pressing her back against it. "Is this okay?"

"Are you inviting me in to continue what we started on the beach?" He loomed over her, his body as close as possible without actually touching. She wanted touching.

"Yes." Her voice came out breathy. "That and more."

He leaned all the way in then, all lips and tongue and groping hands. Her key card fell from her fingers and somehow, he caught it and opened the door without breaking their kiss. Nice move. Although she was certain there were better ones yet to come.

Chapter 12

Lacey woke to Sean's gentle snoring. His body pressed into her back in the cozy bed, and he'd thrown an arm around her waist. Her panic had a hard time spooling up in the hangover haze, but it existed.

If she moved, he'd wake up, and they'd have to face what they'd done. Oh god, the things they'd done. A warm flush flowed through her body at the memories. He'd learned a few things since they'd last been together. Whatever she'd have to face going forward, last night was worth it.

She gently lifted his arm and slid out of bed. He groaned but didn't seem to wake.

She slipped into the bathroom, did her business, and brushed her teeth. Then she chugged two cups of water and two aspirin. Despite the headache, she didn't look too bad. She put on a layer of face cream, brushed her hair, then headed back out. When she reentered the room, Sean stared at her from the bed.

"Should I make some coffee?" she asked, pointing toward the small coffee maker on one of the shelves.

"No. You should come back to bed." He opened the covers for her, and she saw all the reasons why she should, indeed, go back to bed.

"Oh, my god. The restaurant closes in twenty minutes, and I need their strong coffee." Lacey had finally looked at the phone on her nightstand. She rolled toward him one more time, enjoying the velvet of her skin on his and the sated heaviness of her limbs. She gave him a full-lipped kiss. "I'll be out of the shower in five minutes."

"We could shower together." A sly grin crossed his face.

"Not in this shower. I barely fit."

"Fine." A good-natured sigh. "I'll meet you at the restaurant in ten."

Lacey jumped out of bed and headed the three steps to the bathroom.

"Hey," he said. She turned. "You are gorgeous." The smile on his face lit the room.

She slipped into the bathroom, both happy and self-conscious. The last time he'd seen this body, she'd looked a lot better. A lot firmer anyway. And the bodies he'd seen since then, she didn't even want to think about that. But she sure felt beautiful. And well used.

This, she needed more of. The warm water caressed her skin, pouring over the sensitive places that had received the most attention last night. If she didn't need coffee so badly, she'd luxuriate in the shower, take her time with the soap and the lotion.

But coffee called, and she needed to get back to him. She toweled off quickly and left her hair damp. Skin and eye cream she couldn't do without, but other than that, she left her face naked. Whatever this was, it needed to be real, not made-up perfection.

He'd waited for her outside the restaurant, and they entered together. She served herself a coffee, added enough cream to cool it to drinking temperature, and downed the entire cup while standing. Then she poured herself another and got some breakfast.

They sat at a small table near a window on the ocean side of the boat. Not a cloud floated by, and their entire view consisted of light blue sky and dark blue sea. In the brightness of morning, she saw every wrinkle on his face and the specs of gray in his hair. They made him more handsome.

She gazed into his eyes and giggled, remembering all the things they'd done last night.

He wrapped a hand around hers. "I think we're in trouble now."

"Maybe. The kids would freak out." Actually, she couldn't imagine their reactions. Maddie had longed for them to get back together. Even after Sean married someone else.

Zach, being two years younger, responded differently. He thought his dad hung the moon and begged him to come visit every time they talked. It must have wrecked Sean to hear that little boy's voice pitifully crying for his father. Once Sean had another boy, Zach said he wanted to be with his brother. She'd planned to let him stay in Dallas for an entire summer, but he asked to come home after just a few weeks. He must have thought of his brother as a new best friend. Unfortunately, babies don't play. Lacey wished his dreams of family hadn't shattered so early.

"Should we tell the kids?" Sean asked. "I'm not opposed."

"Why don't we keep it between ourselves for now?" A cruise ship affair, a fling, whatever you wanted to call it, wouldn't last.

"I must say, you are making a pretty strong argument for cruise ship living. I could get used to this." He pulled her arm toward him and stroked the tender skin of her wrist."

"I thought you were getting bored?"

"Not anymore. So, what's next? Where are you headed after the scenic coast of Norway?"

Was he serious? And could she handle a retirement with Sean? Cruising with a partner had benefits. Someone to eat with, so you weren't either alone or a third wheel. Someone to sit with on the deck and discuss politics, the weather, or anything else. And last night she'd experienced other benefits up close. But she'd just started this journey and had so much more to explore before anchoring herself to someone.

"I'm not sure where I'm going next. I have a contract on a condo in Oceanside. We're just waiting for my friend's mom to get accepted into an assisted living facility. I assume I'll have to go home to complete that transaction. After that, I was thinking maybe Mexico or the northwest passage." She needed to be more comfortable with their relationship before she'd tell him about the deposit on the Mexico cruise.

"From Seattle to Alaska? Are there fishing options?" He seemed excited. But it had just been one night.

"I'm sure there are, although I hadn't looked into that." They couldn't move this fast, they weren't college kids anymore. "Um, do you think we should give this a little time before we make any plans?"

He stopped stroking her arm. "I can tell you're getting worried. You always get this tightness around your eyes when you worry." He paused, looking a little glum for a moment, then his smile returned. "I don't know what this is. But I've been having a great time with you, and last night was fantastic. I want more. More you. More us. More floating around on a boat with nothing to worry about. Damn, I haven't had a boner like that in years."

"Sean, hush." Lacey looked around to see if anyone had overheard them. The dining room had almost emptied, although one of the waitstaff nearby had a grin a mile wide on his face.

"Lacey, please finish your breakfast. I want to take you back to bed."

At his words, her toes and other important places started tingling. She thought she'd go on a walk after breakfast, then meet him in the viewing room. After that last comment, she couldn't possibly sit beside him for an hour or two without kissing him, pawing him, and other inappropriate acts. Inappropriate for the public anyway.

Heck, the longer she sat at the table, the hornier she got. But a woman needs sustenance. "I'll make you a deal. You go get me another cup of coffee, and I'll shove the rest of the waffle in my face. Then we're going back to bed."

Lacey had never been so forthright, but she wanted him deep down in her bones. Sean jumped up from the table and returned before she'd eaten two bites. He had fresh coffee for both of them and a devilish gleam in his eye.

"So. What exactly am I going to get for coffee duty?" he asked.

Two could play this game. She slipped her foot out of its shoe and her toes worked their way up his pants leg. "I don't know. What would you like?"

His eyes grew big at her maneuver. She wanted to fling her head back and laugh. To be so open and carefree about sex, that had been impossible as a single mom. Her gut and her heart and her bones wanted to make up for all that lost time.

She took one last sip of coffee and stood. "Let's go."

Sean gawked at her. "You may have to walk in front of me. That foot thing—well, it's like I'm eighteen again."

She giggled. When had the world become such a joyous place? They made out in the elevator and then raced each other down the hallway. Every cell in her body glowed with energy, excitement, and fun. She couldn't get enough of retirement.

Chapter 13

Lacey wandered into the viewing room a few minutes late but didn't see Sean at their usual table. She heard him call her name, then saw him waving from a large table near the bow of the ship. Two other couples about their age sat with him.

"Hey, you won't believe it, but I met some people from Texas," he said as she approached.

"Oh, how nice," she said, although she didn't mean it. She'd heard stories about Texans abroad, all loud voices and self-importance.

She'd enjoyed having him all to herself these last few days, and it bummed her out to share him with others. The women caught her eye first. One, an obviously fake redhead given the brightness of each follicle and her age, had a face that looked overly plumped, abraded, and made up. Fortunately, Lacey had put on a little makeup herself, lest she fade into the upholstery in comparison. The redhead sat close to a man who appeared deceptively young with his thick, dark hair and intelligent eyes.

The other couple at the table consisted of a bald man with a scruff of white hair around his dome, and a rangy looking woman with the two-toned blond hair popular among young actresses. Lacey thanked COVID for convincing her to let her hair go gray. The spikey platinum didn't age her the way these women's loudly dyed locks did.

She pasted a smile on her face and promised herself to be less judgmental. Anyone who found their way onto a ship half a world away from Texas had to be somewhat interesting. Sean introduced her first to the dark-haired man, Pete Abbott, and Lacey reached out her hand to shake his.

"Formal, are we?" Pete had a bit of a friendly glint in his eye. Although the woman beside him threw knife blades with hers.

"Awe, Lacey just retired. She's used to running things." Sean tried to recover for her. Okay, no more handshakes out here in the post-job world. She'd have to work on that one. She dropped into a chair, feeling like the dorky kid on the playground.

"Yeah, just a few weeks into civilian life," she said, rolling with the joke.

"This here is Pete's wife Natalie." Sean's Texas twang had become far more noticeable at this table of compatriots. Lacey smiled and waved at the woman.

"And over here, we have Jimmy and Myra Kelly. Jimmy founded the ProTex Real Estate Trust, and everyone here is from Midland."

Trust the real estate guys to sniff each other out. "And what do the rest of you do?" she asked.

"I've got a little pipeline company," Pete said, leaving no doubt that little meant giant and pipeline meant oil.

Lacey looked at Natalie, who stared back at her like she was half-crazed.

"Me? I do volunteer work. I wouldn't have time for a job."

"You do more for our part of Texas than most," Myra said, reaching over to pat Natalie's hand.

"As do you," Natalie replied.

Lacey had sat at the wrong table. Clearly, these ladies lived a life she'd never experienced. Natalie's jacket even looked like real fur, something Lacey hadn't seen in years, and not just because of the nice weather in Southern California.

Suddenly, Sean's hand rested on her thigh, warm and strong. He gave her a squeeze. She took a breath and relaxed into his touch. "I think I'm going to get a drink. Does anyone need anything?"

She escaped to the bar and gave herself a stern talking to. Her social skills didn't need to fly out the window just because she wanted to spend the night alone with

Sean. She had chosen cruise life, which meant meeting new people damn near every day.

When the bartender came by, she ordered a glass of rosé, even though normally she preferred a shot of something. Well, not of aquavit. That stuff took a little too much of the edge off. She took a slug of the wine and then three deep breaths to steady herself.

Why did these two couples bother her so? You couldn't pick your friends on a cruise ship, no one stayed that long. At some point, she needed to consider that more deeply. Lacey always had quality friends, but never much quantity. She considered most people at work to be colleagues, not friends. Usually, they worked for her, or she worked for them, which made for unbalanced friendships.

She could be nice to these people for an evening. They'd become acquaintances, not friends. And if she really wanted to spend the evening with Sean, well, she glanced over at him. He laughed heartily, seeming to enjoy their company.

New attitude in place, she sauntered back to the table and slid into her seat. "That's much better. I'd love to learn more about you and how you ended up in Norway." Her eyes roamed across everyone, but she looked at each of the women a touch longer. What were their stories?

Natalie spoke first. "We go on a cruise together every year. This year Myra chose. I prefer sailboats in the Caribbean. She likes to go crazy places. Two years ago, we took a summer cruise around Iceland."

"Yeah, and in two years, Antarctica." Myra lifted her glass as if in a cheer, but Natalie just shook her head.

"I'm looking forward to that one," Myra's husband said, rubbing her back.

"Why cruises?" Lacey asked. "This is my first one, but I'm intrigued by people choosing to live on cruise ships for their retirement."'

"Oh, I could never do that. I'd miss my kids and my friends. Besides, I can't imagine Peter not working." Natalie placed a diamond-encrusted hand on her husband's arm. Rings, tennis bracelets, hadn't she ever heard of the tragedy of blood diamonds? Doubtful, since she also seemed to wear real fur.

Christ, I'm turning into Maddie. She needed to stop assessing these people she didn't even know.

"I think it sounds kind of exciting, always being on the move." Myra tilted her head, seeming to really consider the question. "Although I can't imagine you ever slowing down enough for that." She directed the comment at her husband.

"I kind of like the life we have. We get away enough." The man's quiet voice had an undercurrent of steel. Husband and wife stared at each other for a moment.

Something passed between the two of them that aroused Lacey's curiosity. Jimmy had seemed deferential to his wife, but Lacey had no doubt he had final say. An odd couple, Lacey bet Myra towered over her husband. In an earlier age, people would have called her homely, although Lacey found her looks interesting. Lacey could imagine her at a company, working as its vice president or even CEO. Something about her seemed strong and serious, the opposite of Natalie's breathy softness. An odd friendship.

"We'd never let the most important finance man in Texas disappear into the seas." This came from Peter.

"I've heard that," said Sean, jumping into the conversation. "You mostly finance oil and gas, right?"

"That's about ninety percent of our business." Jimmy swirled a glass of amber liquid. Whatever tension had briefly existed between him and his wife vanished.

Lacey could tell from the look on his face that Sean was formulating a question that would move the conversation toward commercial real estate. She jumped in first.

"Do you ever fund renewable energy projects?" she asked.

Jimmy gave her an intense look, not unlike the one he'd given his wife. "We used to, but now we focus on oil and gas. Renewables no longer have the support of the Texas government."

"Why on earth not?" Incredulous, Lacey's comment came out sharp. Sean put a hand on her arm like he used to do to calm her down.

"Renewables wouldn't survive without subsidies. Texas is an oil state, always has been. The right people realized this and are rolling back some of the renewable energy incentives."

"But what about climate change? The only chance we have at stopping it is by ending our reliance on fossil fuels."

Jimmy stood. "Honey, you have no idea what you're talking about, and I'm not going to ruin my vacation by listening to this crap. Come on, Myra. It's time to leave."

Myra and Natalie stood at the same time. Peter rose more slowly. "Didn't you say you wanted to retire to a cruise ship? You clearly have no idea how bad they are for the environment. Sometimes it's best not to preach at others when you have wood in your own eye."

She watched them walk away. They didn't relocate to another table but left the viewing room as if they couldn't be present in the same space as her.

"What the fuck?" Sean's harsh whisper reached her, and she turned.

"Seriously? You're blaming me. Have you ever listened to our children? Please tell me you believe in climate change."

Sean sighed as if the weight of everything their kids feared had dropped onto his shoulders. "I believe in climate change. But I don't believe in pissing off people you've just met."

"Why? Because you see them as future business deals?"

"Maybe. What's wrong with that?"

"You don't think that compromises your integrity?" She couldn't believe him.

"I think being a bitch to people compromises your integrity." His features turned from angry to shocked, as if he couldn't believe he'd actually said that. "I'm sorry."

She stood, tears stinging her eyes. She wanted to tell him to go to hell. And she wanted to ask him how he could still hurt her like that. But most of all, she wanted to flee, so she did.

Chapter 14

Lacey hadn't reached her room before the waterworks started. The interaction with the Texans stung, but the comment from Sean had slapped her in the face. She thrust her keycard against the pad so hard she broke a nail. Damn it.

She grabbed her nail file, but by the time she dropped to the couch, her tears blinded her. Why had she come here, so far away from everything familiar? She sank into the embarrassment of the evening and the sadness of no longer having a home.

Eventually, she had to stop crying. No one would comfort her. She half hoped Sean would stop by, but then, he'd been the one to crack the dam of tears.

They'd spent every night together since that first one. Would he come tonight? Or would he find the Texans and dine and drink with them late into the night? She had no power over his decisions.

She got up and washed her face and drank a glass of water. Then, she reached for her computer. She couldn't control what others did, but she could research the environmental effects of cruise ship travel. Peter's words had scalded her. She couldn't very well throw stones at others' climate transgressions if her whole way of life threatened the very house she called home.

What she found was ugly. Especially cruises to Alaska. She read an interactive article that detailed how the waste from ships dirtied the sea. Cruise ships also caused issues among the First Nations and impacted animal life. By the time she finished reading, the information had caused a pit to open in her belly for all the wrong happening in the world. The cruise ship industry embodied everything her children fought against.

So, where did that leave her?

She had the condo in Oceanside. Perhaps she should return there and figure out the future. But it was one thing to think of the condo as a waystation, a place she could land between exotic trips, and a home where she truly wanted to live for the next twenty years. She sighed, heavy and deep, just as the ship's horn blew.

For the first time, she missed TV. She wanted something to entertain her so she wouldn't have to think anymore. There was just too much to consider. She pulled out her iPad to cue up a movie. December hadn't arrived yet, but she needed something hopeful and fun. *Love Actually*. Why not, Christmas would come eventually. And where would she be for the holidays? She couldn't have the kids to the condo with only one extra bedroom. Maybe she could rent a house in the Bay Area and host Christmas there. Would Sean be a part of the celebration?

Too many thoughts and too much still unknown. She fixed herself a bowl of granola and pressed play.

Lacey woke alone the next morning and made coffee in her room before heading out on her morning walk around the ship. No Sean. That just meant she needed to get on with her life. No being lonely.

She wanted a tough workout today, something that would tire her body and perhaps quiet her mind. She started by trotting down the stairs to the lowest level of the ship. The levels below the waterline must hold cargo and perhaps the ship's quarters, although she couldn't verify this because of keypad locks at the doors.

Taking the stairs, she huffed herself up to the highest level, again guarded by locked doors. Given what she'd seen when she looked at the ship from the outside, she imagined the captain behind the locked door, overseeing the ship's operations and staring out into the blue beyond.

Bent over with her hands on her thighs for support, Lacey spent a minute catching her breath, her lungs heaving. Once her breathing had returned to something resembling normal, she ran a sleeve across her damp forehead. Time to head outside.

Her favorite deck had a walkway around the entire ship. At the rear of the boat, visitors often congregated on the large, flat observation deck.

Lacey planned on circling the deck as many times as it took for exhaustion to set in, but on her first pass, she saw Krista leaning against the deck's back rail. An orange glow shot through a space where slate gray clouds had parted. Sunrise.

Lacey joined her and rested her forearms on the railing, mimicking Krista's position. "Good morning. Where's your mom?" Lacey hadn't seen them apart before.

"She wasn't feeling well after breakfast, so I took her back to the room. It's nice to have a few minutes on my own." Krista sounded worn out, while Lacey, despite the stairs, hummed with worried energy.

Everything that happened last night, from the unpleasant conversation with the Texans to Sean not coming to her cabin and her research on cruises whirled around her head, obscuring her path forward. She had to stop. She closed her eyes and took a deep breath. When she opened them again, tangerine and fuchsia rays burst from the break in the clouds like the coming of a neon angel.

"Oh, wow. That is so beautiful." The bright lights mesmerized Lacey as they shifted, painting snowy mountains pink and apricot and striping the ocean periwinkle and amethyst. Finally, a pale gold disk pushed its way through the rosy hues, overtaking them with brightness.

"The world is an incredible place," Krista said. She might have spoken the words to Lacey, but they seemed more like a statement left at the feet of a Norse god.

"I'm not sure I've ever seen anything so beautiful." Lacey's inner voice stilled, allowing her to enjoy the moment.

"I have. A newborn, an elegant deer caught unaware on a forest path, meadows full of wildflowers. My beautiful mother." Krista's soft voice trembled at the final words.

Lacey turned to her. "I'm so sorry. Is your mom sick?"

"No." The woman's head shook slowly. "Well, she's got lots of conditions that make life harder, but she's not supposed to drop dead anytime soon. We decided that this would be our last trip together. The travel is just too hard."

Lacey hadn't thought about becoming too old to cruise. After all, elevators whisked one up and down at the bow and stern of the ship. You could sit around all day, and someone cleaned your room and prepared your meals.

"A cruise seems like the perfect idea. I've looked into cruise ship retirement. Although someone at dinner last night gave me a hard time about the environmental impacts." Maybe the turmoil of last night made her open up to an almost stranger, although Krista's caring nature had something to do with it. Lacey watched the foaming wake of the ship's propellers stretch behind them, such a pretty sign of fossil fuel consumption.

Krista let out a heavy sigh. "No one person can stop climate change. That's a myth the big oil companies have sold us to shift the blame from them to us."

Lacey brightened at Krista's words. Maybe she'd bought into a story and didn't have to accompany her decisions with remorse. But if no one changed, the climate crisis would continue to worsen. "Don't we have to make things better, reverse climate change?"

Krista looked at her, a deep sadness in her eyes. "You can't reverse climate change. We're too far down that path." She pointed out to sea, to the north as they traveled south. "The arctic melt can't be reversed. It's the same with the glaciers. The life that depends on them, polar bears, reindeer, and lots of less glamorous species, they're already gone. You can only hope to slow the coming disaster. Make it a little less terrible."

"What do you mean the polar bears are gone?"

"Ice at the arctic circle is breaking up and melting. Polar bears use that ice to hunt prey, primarily seals. Already, so much ice has melted that sometimes it's too far for the bears to swim from one sheet to another. Someday soon the summer ice won't exist. The bears don't walk on water and without ice can't get to their prey. They'll starve."

"It's really that bad?" It hurt the way it had hurt when her childhood dog died—pain too sharp to breathe through.

"I'm sorry, but yes." The devastated look in Krista's eyes mirrored Lacey's heart.

The dire words pounded their way through her. It couldn't be. Lacey wanted to throw up. "So you just give up? There's no hope for the future?"

Something fierce took hold of her heart, lit a spark of anger as she looked at the cold northern sea. Lacey had spent her life solving problems. How could she just give up? Her children didn't deserve such a fated world. "Is everyone supposed to eat steak every day, drive SUVs, and live on cruise ships?"

Krista chuckled, but there was no joy in it. "I don't think you'll need an SUV on a cruise ship, although that's an apt illustration of a gross carbon footprint. And no, doing nothing isn't a solution. Making change happen in communities, nationally, internationally—that's where our best hope lies. Why not become vegan or drive an all-electric vehicle? Every positive change helps the looming disaster become a tiny bit less terrible. But systemic change is what's needed. So, if you want to take your mother on a cruise because it's the only way she can enjoy a vacation, I say go for it."

Lacey hadn't meant to sound selfish, hadn't meant to accuse Krista when she cared about her own blame in this fiasco, not someone else's. The enormity of the other woman's ideas had blasted a hole in her chest. She thought hope existed, but that dream had turned into a terrifying void.

The women stood in silence, looking out at the water and coast passing them by. The ship chugged past an island where a crag of rock shot straight up out of the ocean. A perfect circle of nothingness cut through the center of the stone like a looking glass. If she jumped off the boat and swam to it, could she crawl through that hole to a better world?

The once beautiful scenery turned bleak. If Krista were right, everything she saw would be just a figment of imagination for the generations after her. It was already gone. But she knew that. She knew about sea level rise. The sea would inundate the cute towns with the quaint brightly colored houses. She just hadn't realized what that truly meant before.

"I better go and check on Mom," Krista said.

"I might as well just throw myself off the back of the boat. I never realized how truly screwed we were until now." She didn't mean it, but she couldn't help the jab. Lacey hadn't been entirely ignorant, but it had certainly felt like bliss compared to this.

"I'm sorry. I just think we need to face reality and stop thinking climate change isn't so bad."

"I met some people last night who don't even think it exists."

"Really? I've found that those people usually get it, they just want to profit from the sinking ship as it goes down." With that, Krista left the deck, and left Lacey mired in sadness about the end of the world.

She wandered around her favorite walking path one more time, not exercising this time, just trying to figure things out. Yesterday, she'd preached about climate change to others, yet today Krista's comments had shifted the world beneath her feet.

What was her role in a coming disaster? Her project management mind wanted to look at the data and figure a way to a brighter future. But she couldn't make the columns align. Krista's prognosis left her reeling.

Lacey gave up and made her way back to her cabin. She wanted to crawl beneath the sheets and forget the conversation had ever taken place. She opened the door to a piece of paper at her feet. Scrawled on the ship's stationery was an *I'm sorry, can we talk? S.*

Her heart squeezed. She'd enjoyed the sex, really enjoyed it. But the companionship had made the relationship special. However, even in her most relaxed and intimate moments with Sean, she never thought of their relationship as long-term.

He'd always have a piece of her heart, and he'd always be her friend. They'd shared too much in their lives, including their wonderful children. Regrettably, they also had a long track record of disappointing each other, and she could see that happening again and again. He still wanted to live in Dallas, to prove himself in real estate. He probably still had a taste for buxom younger women.

Lacey hadn't been sure of her path before, but the conversation with Krista had completely unmoored her. Part of her wanted to cling to Sean, or anything from her past. But that kind of holding on wouldn't save her. According to Krista, nothing would. But, of course, nothing would anyway. From birth, every person traveled on a journey toward death. She'd always known that. She just didn't think she'd take the rest of the world with her.

Still, it wasn't like she could crawl into the corner, curl up, and die. Humans didn't do that. Like cockroaches, they had an incredible ability to adjust.

Lacey stepped into the bathroom and washed her face. She carefully applied her makeup, even spritzed on a little perfume. Then she grabbed her book and her room key and headed to the viewing deck.

Sean sat at their favorite nook. He stood as she approached, and she saw he'd ordered her a club soda with extra lime. Most of its ice had melted. He'd waited a while for her. She gave him a grin.

He leaned into her and whispered, "I'm sorry," before kissing her cheek. "I was a complete ass last night."

She didn't disagree. "Where are your friends today?"

"I think they're touring the bridge, then having a private lunch with the captain."

He'd probably had breakfast with them but hadn't been invited on their special tour. That meant he left her the note when he had nothing to do. She wasn't proud of thinking the worst of him, but he'd disappointed her before.

"They aren't people our children would like." Lacey launched the comment, the first salvo in an attempt, if not to find common ground, at least to figure out where they both stood.

"You didn't seem to like them too much either."

Lacey sat with the comment for a minute. If the whole fucking world was burning, why be polite? "No. I thought they were pretentious, catty, and fake."

A look of shock crossed Sean's face. She enjoyed getting under his skin. She offered a lopsided grin.

"You know, people can have different views and still get along," Sean said.

"Do you even believe in climate change?"

"Of course. I'm not an idiot. Even I see the weather changing."

"It's not just about the weather. And we need to stop fossil fuel production to have an impact on it. Those are oil industry guys. Do you think they'll ever agree to that?"

Sean steepled his fingers. His tell when uncomfortable. "I'm not sure we need to go that far."

She closed her eyes and let the sadness flow through her. Then, she looked deep into his dark eyes, searching for all the things she had loved in him. "Do you believe our children or Texas politicians? Even more importantly, who would you choose?"

"Our children. Always."

"They don't just believe in climate change, they're spending their lives battling it and the injustice it's based on."

"I understand that. I truly do. But what am I supposed to do? Quit my job and become a climate warrior? That doesn't make any sense." He leaned back and glanced at the bar.

Lacey also craved a drink, thought it would smooth the conversation. But she didn't want to stop their progress. Not yet.

"I don't have any solutions. I'm still trying to figure out what my role is. Zach suggested doing something with some of the proceeds from the house. I was so tired of them always bugging me about this stuff that I didn't even listen to him. I should have." She saw that now.

"But don't you need that money for your retirement? You have to make sure you're taken care of. Besides, I've donated to their causes for years. We've done our share."

"There's no "share" big enough to make up for all we've done wrong."

"You can't believe that. We worked hard. I'm in real estate, you're in medical devices. Those aren't big pollution industries."

His words sounded so logical. But she understood now that the crisis went far deeper than that. Something about her conversation with Krista had seeped into her, changing the composition of her cells, until she realized Krista was right. The crisis loomed over them like the end of the world.

"We've destroyed the planet," she said. "We did. Our parents did. Our grandparents. For generations, we've spewed carbon into the atmosphere, and now it's too late to stop the glaciers from melting, the oceans from warming. We've killed so much." Her voice trembled with its new death warrant.

"Hang on. It's not that bad yet."

"It is," she said. "Our kids have told us this over and over. I just didn't listen before. But now, seeing this place, listening to the woman studying whales and other people—I finally get it."

"We've got time. I can go back to Texas, live another twenty or thirty years, and everything will be fine. Maybe it will be hotter. Maybe we'll have a few more hurricanes, lose a few inches of beach, but I don't live on the coast. I don't think it is the emergency you believe it is, although I agree that our kids are in a tougher situation."

He might be right. Dallas might not burn or wash away. But much of the Texas coast might. She thought of Hurricane Katrina, of the horrible flooding off the coast of Spain. So many storms these days were the worst in history.

"You're not going to lose a few inches of beach. Climate change doesn't work like that. It's not like moving your towel back a foot or two when the tide comes in. Mother Nature is going to be as violent with us as we've been clearcutting her forests and turning her mountains into minerals. Storms will probably wipe out Galveston, Padre Island, the Florida peninsula." She hadn't spoken words like that before. Did they come from her conversation with Krista or from some melding of the news and her daughter's proclamations over the years?

Desperation, sadness, and fear coursed through her with this newly recognized knowledge.

"If it comes to that, I'll help however I can," Sean said. "But honestly, if Turtle Creek floods, my home will be fine. I can get solar panels to run my A/C, maybe even one of those whole-house batteries in case the grid goes down. But people have talked about climate change for a long time and not that much has changed in my world."

All those books Lacey read about privilege during COVID came roaring back to her consciousness. As long as you had a lot of money and not so many years ahead, you could live out your life in relative comfort. The climate crisis might make you sad. Maybe you'd spend a few dollars or a little compassion on those less fortunate. But things didn't really have to change.

"And your kids. What kind of world are you leaving for them?"

He crossed his arms and looked at the verdant coastline, seeming to dwell on the issue. "Maybe we need to set them up, buy them property in a place that will be less affected by climate change. I've heard about billionaires doing that. We could buy them a farm in Maine, or wherever they can best ride it out. I bet Maddie knows the safest places."

"And our son who advocates for social justice? Do you think he'll be content to take the rich man's way out?" Lacey tried to bleed the oxygen from the spark of anger that lit in her chest. She wanted to keep him talking. She had no more answers than he did, and the entire world needed these conversations. Besides, the desire to find a way to protect her particular children from the coming disaster was as natural as offering a breast to her crying baby. Privilege or not, she wanted them to survive.

"Damn it, Lacey. I don't have all the answers. I wish I did. You know, I didn't cause this problem." Tense muscles moved along his jaw and he ran a hand roughly through his hair.

"No, those assholes you pandered to last night did." She inhaled and briefly closed her eyes. That wasn't the whole truth. "And we did. We just didn't understand the consequences of our actions."

He pulled a hand through his hair, exasperation written across his features. "I don't want to fight with you. We just found each other again. Can't we just have some fun? Maybe see if this thing between us can go somewhere?"

His offer tore her heart in two. Not because she'd take him up on it, but because it offered a path forward when she hadn't figured hers out yet. Instead of loneliness, it promised companionship with someone she truly liked. And mostly, it would give her something sure when all the world seemed ready to burst into flames.

"How about you buy me a bourbon? I don't think we're going to figure out how to save the planet today, but let's keep talking. We may need a friend at the end of the world."

Later that evening, Lacey found Krista and asked if she could join them for dinner. She saw Sean across the dining room at a table with the Texans. She'd enjoyed her earlier drink with him, and the conversation, although she found him somewhat infuriating. He admitted a problem existed but planned on running on that flat tire until he ground the rim down to the axle.

She didn't invite him back to her room. A part of her wanted that physical comfort, but she couldn't afford the price. Getting attached to him again would hurt just as much as the first time when it didn't work out. And it wouldn't. Lacey couldn't see the path in front of her, but they weren't traveling the same road.

At dinner she had the salmon, for what seemed like the ninth time in eight days. Although delicious, once she'd gone through the menu, the options became less appealing. Perhaps this signaled yet another issue with cruise life.

"Is that your husband over there with those other people?" Krista asked.

"Hmph." The vocalization came from Krista's mother, Olga, and said more than words ever could.

Lacey rubbed her face with her hands. She didn't enjoy having to explain the lie. Although she preferred it to eating dinner with the Texans. "He's my ex-husband. We divorced years ago."

"But . . ." Krista's confused look embarrassed Lacey. "You looked so happy together. So in love."

Lacey's cheeks went hot. "He surprised me by showing up in Trondheim, and we, well, we kind of hit it off." Christ. How could she possibly explain this without sounding like a slut?

"Aah." Olga said, telling Lacey she understood exactly what had happened. "The sex is good."

"Mother!"

Olga shrugged her shoulders. "It is what it is. You should find someone like that."

"I'm so sorry." Now Krista blushed. "She's been disappointed since I divorced my first husband thirty-five years ago."

"He was no good." Olga took a healthy sip from a glass of red wine.

"I never noticed your accent before. Where are you from?" Lacey asked. The older woman just shrugged.

"She's from Russia, via Brazil. But it's only recently that her accent has gotten stronger. She sounds more like my grandmother than my mother these days." Krista said the words with a smile on her face, but Lacey saw worry lines as well. Olga had to be in her late eighties. Lacey wished her own mother had made it that long.

"If you don't mind my asking, what happened tonight?" Krista raised an eyebrow in Sean's direction, just as their table burst into loud Texas laughter.

What happened? Everything. Nothing. She settled on a response. "I'm not a fan of the company he's keeping."

"They do seem a little extra," Krista said.

Lacey stifled a giggle. Tonight, the redhead wore a scarlet suede jacket with rhinestones and fringe, and the blond had on a leopard print dress that showed the entirety of her substantial cleavage. It almost surprised her that the men hadn't donned cowboy boots and spurs. Sometimes you could spot the Texans a mile away.

"Yeah. Plus, the climate change conversation you and I had on the deck was a real eye-opener. Sean and I talked about it as well. I wouldn't call him a skeptic, but he doesn't think he'll have to worry about it in his lifetime."

Olga just shrugged, but Krista seemed to consider the statement. "Doesn't Texas have pretty shitty weather? Like hurricanes and droughts and things?"

"Yes," Lacey said. "But he thinks his money will protect him."

"It won't protect him from climate refugees. Texas has a long border with Mexico. We're already seeing droughts in Mexico and Central America sending desperate people north just to survive. I'm not sure how many will stay in Texas, especially since points north are better for agriculture, at least for now. But there's going to be a lot of desperate people passing through his neighborhood."

The prospect made her head hurt. Texas's governor already hated immigrants so much he'd placed floating barriers laced with razor wire across the Rio Grande. The deathtraps had done their jobs, killing several people before the federal government put an end to the torture.

"I don't know," Lacey said. "Texas is pretty tough on immigrants." She picked at her salmon, wishing the world were a better place.

"People desperate to save themselves and their children are going to come. They don't have a choice."

As a mom, Lacey would do anything to protect her kids. Any mother would. "I think it might get ugly."

"No doubt, although we're far luckier than Europeans," Krista said.

"It's true." Olga agreed with her daughter.

"What do you mean?" Lacey asked, although she feared the answer as much as she wanted to hear it.

"All of Asia, the Middle East, and Africa have fairly easy access to Europe. Their climate refugee crisis will be dire."

That made twice today that Krista had made Lacey's heart hurt so badly she wanted to rip it from her chest. What could they do? What could anyone do? Her children couldn't solve these issues. No one could.

She didn't want to speak, because she feared bursting into tears. It all seemed so hopeless. Why even try? Why not just be like Sean and say *fuck it*? She had enough money to live out the rest of her years in relative comfort. After that, she wouldn't have to deal with any of it.

"How do you even go on in the face of all that tragedy?" Lacey asked.

"There aren't a lot of choices." Krista blew a lock of gray-blond hair off her forehead. "You can be like your ex and not care if you make it worse for those who come after you, or you can decide to do something about it. Once you know, you know, and there's no going back on understanding climate change."

Yeah. That was the problem. Just weeks ago, Lacey had thought her retirement years would be the best adventure ever. Now, she almost wanted to go back to when bad bosses were her biggest problems. But that bridge had burned, and she couldn't blame the climate. She'd definitely lit that match.

Plus, earlier in the day, she'd received multiple emails that the closing on her home had gone through. She'd planned on celebrating the boost it gave her bank account. Days ago, she'd imagined opening a bottle of champagne under a twilight sky with Sean by her side. Some things didn't turn out the way you planned.

When the waiter stopped by to take their dessert order from the fixed menu choices, all three of them chose cloudberries and cream. She asked the others if they'd share a bottle of sparkling wine with her.

"I'm having a celebration of sorts. I just sold my house."

"Congratulations, but where will you live now?" Krista asked.

Lacey explained about the condo. The waiter returned with long stemmed glasses he filled with shimmering bubbles. He set pots of white froth speckled with golden berries in front of them. Lacey looked into the kind faces of the women across from her. Sometimes plans change for the better.

"How do you know about all this environmental stuff?" she asked Krista. "I mean, I know you volunteer for an environmental organization, but everyone on this ship seems to know more about climate change than me."

"Americans." Olga shook her head in disdain.

"The rest of the planet thinks about climate change more than we do. They're either living it, with oceans threatening their homelands, along with droughts, blizzards, and crop failures, or they know what's coming and are trying to figure out how to mitigate it. The US still has a huge number of climate deniers, and too few people willing to learn and do more to build a better future."

Well, that put a damper on the celebration. Lacey would go back to Carlsbad, regroup, and figure out the future from there. Maybe instead of a cruise ship, she'd retire to Mexico. She'd had friends who'd done that. Although one couple had come back after a year, loving it for a few months, and then growing bored.

She didn't have to decide anything tonight. Lacey poured the last of the wine. Only a small amount remained, a sip for each woman.

"Thank you," Lacey said, lifting her glass to the others. "It was a pleasure to eat with you tonight."

Normally, after dinner, she would have retired to the viewing deck for a night-cap. Tonight, certain Sean and the loud Texans had beat her there, she returned to her cabin.

She pulled out a book but found her mind wandering to her conversation with Sean. Would she talk to him about refugees, maybe convince him how near the crisis loomed? But did it? He could be right. Maybe he'd spend the next twenty or thirty years watching storms from afar without ever feeling a personal pinch.

She sunk into her morose thoughts. Instead of reading, she slipped on head-phones, queued up her favorite blues albums. The tunes from the last century would pull her deeper into her darkness, but she'd find beauty there also. If only that would happen in the real world as well.

Chapter 15

The ringing tormented her. Lacey crawled out of the deep sleep she'd fallen into before realizing her phone caused the noise. She searched for the device, finding it under her hip. She forced herself to focus on the glare of the screen. Deb's name scrolled across the phone, and it was just past midnight.

"Hello?" She croaked out the word.

"Lacey. Is that you? Are you okay?" Deb asked, sounding hundreds of miles away.

"Yeah. I'm good." Lacey sat up, her head immediately torturing her with a pounding throb. "Too much champagne, not enough sleep".

"I'm sorry," Deb said, her voice cracking. "But my mom died. They found her this morning."

"Oh, no." The pain in her friend's voice pulled Lacey awake. "I'm so sorry to hear that. What happened?"

"They. . . she. Just a minute. I promised myself I'd stop crying." The noise from the phone became muffled.

Poor Deb. When Lacey's parents died, she'd had plenty of time to prepare. Cancer, Alzheimer's, neither killed quickly. Although a surprise death that shocked the living might be better than the long, drawn-out kind.

"Sorry," Deb said, coming back on the call. "There was a fire. They think she left the stove on in her remodeled kitchen. They haven't done an autopsy yet, but they found her in her bedroom. She probably died of smoke inhalation in her sleep."

"I'm so sorry." What else could one say? What a shitty thing to have happened. Lacey couldn't help but wonder how bad the fire was and what kind of damage had happened to the condo.

She should have more compassion for her friend instead of worrying about herself. "What can I do to help?"

"Nothing. Except, your broker is going to ask you to cancel the contract to buy the house. You should. You don't have insurance on it yet, and Mom does. Did. However, you're supposed to say it."

Lacey heard the anguish in Deb's voice, and her heart broke for her friend. "Sure. Whatever's best. I wish I were there to help. The cruise ends in two days. I'm coming home after that."

"Really, I'm fine. You should stay there. The kids are coming home tomorrow, and they'll be here at least through the funeral. I can't even offer you a place to stay."

"Please don't worry about me. You need to focus on your family and take care of yourself right now."

"I will. I'm sorry, but I've got to go." Deb's voice cracked again, and then the phone went dead.

Holy shit. Poor Deb.

Lacey found two aspirins in her carryon, then crawled back under the covers. She forced her eyes closed but couldn't stop her mind from spinning. She had no home. What would she do next? Where would she go? If she'd signed up for an around-the-world cruise, at least she'd have a plan. Although now, with her expanded knowledge about cruises and climate change, she had no desire to go on the weeklong Mexican cruise she'd booked. Her kids worried about the world burning, but instead, it crumbled beneath her feet.

She must have fallen back asleep, because when she next looked at her phone it read four in the morning. A dull nightmare consumed her, asking what she should do and where she belonged?

Lying in bed wouldn't bring answers. She pulled herself up, showered, and washed her face. She had to get out of the tiny cabin too small to contain her worries. Next, she pulled a sweater over yoga pants and layered a boxy fleece on top. She wished she'd brought fuzzy slippers, anything to feel cozy and comfortable. It would combat the loneliness howling at her door.

Not a single person sat on the indoor viewing deck. Fortunately, the ship's staff had prepared a dispenser full of fresh, hot coffee.

She sat at the window, leaning out and looking for light. Nothing. The outside remained as bleak as her prospects. She'd have to start over. But wasn't retirement supposed to be a fresh start? Nothing felt fresh about this morning. Foreboding, yes. Nauseating, yes.

She tried to meditate, taking long breaths and holding her mind still. But it insisted on wandering, wondering what came next. She didn't even know what she wanted. Travel sounded fun when stability wasn't an issue. News of death made her want to cling to her children, but they had their own lives. Maybe she should just stay on this ship, cruising past a dark and silent coast until the future came to her. Although if she listened to kids and pundits, that future would be dire indeed.

She finished her coffee, then filled another mug. She should go back to bed, but it seemed some kind of reckoning had drawn her here. Yet her mind, usually so good at solving problems, at putting plans into place and following them through, had taken its own vacation. And so she sat, almost thoughtless, staring into a black morning sky.

"Lacey?"

She heard him behind her, saw Sean's reflection in the dark window. Lacey peered into her mug, but she'd emptied it long ago. She pressed her phone. Six a.m. Maybe she had entered a meditative state. Somehow, she'd lost time.

"Are you okay?" Sean asked.

"I'm fine." She even sounded fine.

"Are you sure? You don't sound so good."

So much for that. She needed a minute to pull herself back from wherever her mind had gone. "Would you get me a cup of coffee? With cream."

"I remember." He reached for her cup.

Lacey rubbed her hands against her face, hoping to bring a little color to her cheeks. Then she brushed her hands through her hair and took a deep breath. She needed to draw on her strength for this conversation, not break down and admit she felt lost.

"Here you go." Sean set the cup on the table, then took the seat beside her. "Will you tell me what you're thinking?"

They used to ask each other that question. She'd asked it of him, curious and in love. Later, she'd asked it with rage seeping just below the surface. Even later, she didn't need to ask. She'd known he wanted to run out on them. But she asked anyway, just to make him say it. Her mind moved to a few days earlier and how tender he'd been in bed. So many faces in just one person.

"Deb's mom died." Best to start there, with somebody else's pain.

"Oh, no. I'm sorry to hear that. Didn't you tell me you bought her mother's condo?"

Of course he'd remember that detail. Anything to do with property and his mind found it and locked it in. "Yeah, about that. I guess her mom burned the place down, or at least the kitchen." She'd left the Band-Aid half pulled off, the *what's next* end dangling from her tender skin. He'd take the bait.

"Have you already closed on the property? I assume not, since she was living there."

"Correct. Deb says they'll cancel the contract." Nothing. She felt nothing. Had she not wanted to live there? Maybe the loss hadn't sunk in.

"That's good news."

Incensed, she watched him take a sip from his mug. "How is that good? My best friend has lost her mother, and I no longer have a home." Ah, there it was. The missing pain roared in like an angry child.

"I feel terrible for Deb, but you don't need the hassle of rebuilding." The last word died on his tongue.

She almost looked at the window, wondering if her reflection would show how broken she felt. Instead, she closed her eyes and mouth so her feelings couldn't escape.

"Babe, I'm so sorry. Come here." He scooted his chair next to hers, opened his arms to envelop her.

She caved, going all soft and squishy and sad. He held her as the tears leaked from her eyes and the word 'lost' echoed through her mind, plummeted through her heart, and found her soul somewhere near her guts. The job she wanted to leave, her retirement condo, the plans for travel that now seemed obscene. She'd lost them all. Even in Sean's arms, she'd never felt so alone.

Lacey let his warmth seep into her. When she tried to relax, the arm of her chair poked into her.

"Hey, get up for a second. Let's go sit over there." He rose, pulling her up with him, and shuffled her over to a couch.

Lacey dropped to the seat, and his arm never left her. He tucked her into his side, and she rested there, eyes closed.

She must have fallen asleep. When she woke, her head rested on Sean's chest. Their bodies touched all the way to their ankles. She wanted to feel embarrassed about needing him so much, but she couldn't. The interlude of sleeping, completely safe in his arms, had finally stilled her restless mind.

She lifted her head. "Thanks. How long have I been asleep?"

He gave her a quick grin, then kissed her lightly on the forehead. "Just about ten minutes. Not long."

"I remember when we were married, you used to put me to bed when I'd get overwhelmed. You'd stroke my back until I fell asleep, and when I woke, everything seemed a little better." It had infuriated her that a tactic you'd use on a toddler worked on her, but it did.

"Sometimes you'd get those wheels spinning so hard, you couldn't rest. That kind of focus and dedication made you great at your job. But every once in a while, you just needed to take a little time for yourself."

"Thanks. For all those times, and for now." Not everything had worked between them, but in so many ways, he cared for her better than anyone else ever had. All the big changes came with their downsides. Losing Sean, having kids, retiring. She'd missed someone taking care of her, even while she wanted her freedom.

And now? She'd lost her purpose. Looking forward to retiring for so many years, she'd overlooked the downsides. Now, she had to find a reason to get up in the morning, whether it was travel, tai chi, gardening, or any of the myriad of activities retirees engaged in. That, combined with her growing understanding of the tragedy of climate change, and then the blow of losing the home she hadn't even had the chance to occupy, had dragged her to the edge of the abyss. Fortunately, Sean had been there to hold on to her and make sure she didn't fall in.

She would need community in her future. Whether or not she liked them, and she had liked most of them, her coworkers had formed a community. Perhaps the absence of community had made it easier to fall for Sean all over again.

Her anger at herself for inviting him back into her life, only to let him hurt her again, had taken root without her noticing. Now she brought that emotion out into the open, acknowledged its presence, and told herself it was okay. She wasn't twenty anymore. She could be disappointed in him, and in herself, and still appreciate how he'd found her this morning when she needed exactly what he had to offer.

"You came along at just the right moment," she said. "And I am so grateful for that."

Surprise crossed his face. She should have told him that more often back then. Although, it wouldn't have changed the outcome.

"I'm glad I could be here for you." He didn't say *this time* or *like I should have been*, but she could see it in his eyes.

"I think I'll head back to my cabin. The ship is supposed to dock at Ålesund this morning, and I want to hike to the viewpoint." She'd read about the strenuous walk up 418 steps and had planned on avoiding it. Now it sounded like the perfect antidote to her discontent.

"Would you like company?" Sean asked.

"Maybe not today. I've got some thinking to do." While she appreciated his urge to help, she wanted to strike out alone. She needed to figure out her future on her own.

The city spread beneath her on a spit of land with fingers jutting into the water in every direction. Buildings covered almost every scrap of flat rock. Sheer cliffs of multicolored wooden structures rose from the water's edge. Across from the city, giant rocky hills jutted from the sea. To her right, a soccer stadium seemed perched atop the sea.

The small city nestled in the fjords proved how man could coexist with nature. At least for now. She took photo after photo, each more fascinating than the last. She wished she could spend the afternoon here, maybe twenty-four hours or more. But the boat would leave the dock in ninety minutes, and then they'd arrive in Bergen, the final stop, thirty-six hours later.

The hike up the town's mountain had done its job, alleviating her anxiety until the reality of the cruise ending hit her like barreling into a wall. Maybe she would come back here. Maybe she'd stay in Bergen. She'd planned a few days in Oslo, but now she literally had nowhere to go.

She fled down the mountain with its cold air and harsh reality. Every time she pulled herself out of the morass, something shoved her back down. But she was a grown woman, and she would figure her way into the future. She needed to put her project manager's hat back on, look at her options, and make a decision.

Where to live, what to do—she could solve these problems. Unlike many, she had tools like money and time that would ease her way.

She trod up the ramp with determination and reboarded the ship, fixated on getting her life in order. At her room, she spied a note under the door. An invitation, a plea actually, from Sean. He wanted to have dinner with her tonight at the high-end restaurant.

The invitation didn't leave her time to problem solve. Instead, she showered and pulled on the only dress she hadn't worn yet, a dusky blue velvet the color of the sky after the sun had set, or the ocean on a cloudy day. She'd bought it because she thought it matched her eyes, a dark blue-gray that she'd inherited from a long line of women on her mother's side of the family.

The hike had turned her cheeks pink, and she didn't look bad for sixty. Sometimes dressing up the outside supplied confidence missing on the inside. Eyeliner, mascara, and lipstick completed the look. She'd have loved pretty heels and fancy earrings, but a person could only pack so much.

For work, she often wore a severe suit or bold colors, especially when she had an important meeting. Power dressing signaled self-assurance, spoke of control without having to say anything. Tonight was the same. She wanted to be all the things she didn't feel inside.

Lacey arrived ten minutes late. Sean waited for her outside the restaurant, looking handsome in a navy blazer and charcoal slacks. He beamed when he saw her.

"You look amazing. What a difference a few hours makes."

She'd dressed up for him, she realized. Not to seduce him, but to tell him she'd recovered. He didn't need to worry about her anymore. He'd done his part.

They ordered, and he asked if they could start with champagne. He seemed nervous, all movement and short sentences. It put her on edge. He'd acted the same way when he used to talk to her about moving back to Texas. He'd decided something and wanted her to go along.

The waiter delivered the champagne, and he clinked her glass with a quick "cheers." Then he played with his fork, twirling it under the ceiling light.

She put her hand on top of his to still its movement. "Just tell me."

"I know you don't have any place to go." He looked up at her and almost winced. At least he realized he could have started in a better way. "We pull into Bergen late tomorrow. It's supposed to be an incredible city. My secretary found an Airbnb with a terrace that has a gorgeous view of the harbor and the city. She booked it for seven days. Why don't we stay there? It will give you a chance to figure out what to do next."

Lacey's eyebrows rose so high her eyes felt tight. They hadn't slept together since before the Texas incident and now he assumed she wanted to share a room with him??

"It's got two bedrooms," he said. "You'd have your own space. It also has a kitchen and living room and an incredible stone terrace looking over the city. I need to do some thinking too, or I should say you've inspired me to examine my life. I thought if we did it together, we could help each other out."

Lacey took a long sigh, buying time. "As friends?"

"Yeah. I'm really sorry about how I handled the Texans. I didn't mean to piss you off. Sometimes I just go into business mode and screw over the people who are important. It's one of the things I need to think about. My partners have complained about it before."

"Really?" She found his openness unusual, for any man.

"Yeah, and it's not like those guys were going to do business with me. They've already got people for anything I can do." He gave her a sly smile. "And you are way more fun to hang out with."

She couldn't imagine what meal after meal with those catty women had been like. And she liked the men even less.

"Your offer is intriguing," she finally said. "But as you saw this morning, I've got a lot to work through."

"Let me be there for you. I wasn't before, but I can be now. I want to be. I want us to be there for each other." His sincerity charmed her. It always had, but she wouldn't slip back into the mess they'd made earlier.

"As friends?" she asked again.

"As friends." A smile lit his eyes, and he chuckled softly. "Unless and until you want something more."

He might not stop trying to get back into her bed, but his offer would give her a little breathing room. "Let's give it a shot."

Chapter 16

Lacey looked out from the stone terrace as Bergen glowed golden in the setting sun. She'd loved the city from the moment they chugged into the bay. One side of the bay gleamed with peaked-roof, multi-story buildings built centuries earlier that tilted into each other. Their bright colors and giddy sagging reminded her of girlfriends coming home together after a night of drinking.

Buildings and roads covered every inch of semi-flat land near the water before the sides of the fjord rose steeply toward the sky. Set off by the verdant cliffs, shiny black and terracotta roofs caught the light. A floating wharf held a farmer's market and colorful restaurants. Boats filled the bay, from giant cruise ships to tiny water taxis. The water seemed as busy as a California freeway.

The beautiful city and cool air should have been the perfect place to sort out her dreams. But staring down upon the glorious city, her eyes kept seeing violent storms and rising water. None of this would survive.

Sean came up beside her and handed her a cup of tea. Right place. Right person?

"Thanks. So, what are your thoughts about your future?" she asked.

"I don't know how I'd fill my days if I retired. But I'm not going to lie, the company is pressuring me to leave. They have so many solid people and there's no way for them to move up unless I make room."

"Fuck 'em. You earned your place. Although do you want to sit in an office for the rest of your life?"

They stared at the city as the sky darkened and lights popped on in buildings along the bay. The reflection in the water made them twice as bright.

"That's the rub," he finally said. "I'm supposed to want something different, but all I can think of is sitting in my big house all alone instead of in an office filled with people."

"You need a wife."

"Are you applying for that position?"

Lacey heard the joke in his voice but wanted to set him straight, just in case. "There's no fucking way. I'd never move back to Texas, and even though we've had our fun here, I think we both know it would never work."

"Indulge me for a moment. Why wouldn't it work? You're someone I can talk to about big issues. You're smart, beautiful, the whole package. I wish I hadn't lost you the first time around."

She took a sip of tea, some herbal blend they'd found in a cabinet. "I don't think I'm going to put up with people who don't believe in climate change anymore. It seems like that's the least I owe my children."

"But I told you, I do believe. But I don't control it. We're at the end of our lives. What choice do we have except to hope human ingenuity comes to the rescue? I won't be the one to find that solution, or solutions. I'm just an old real estate guy."

An urge struck to throw her tea at him. Maybe that would wake him up. She forced her hands still. The word disaster looped through her head like a fire alarm. She couldn't just sit back and wait until someone else put out the fire. Not when her children lived in the building. Yet, like Sean, she had no power to fix the issue.

She wanted to beat her head against a wall, to cry, to wallow. But that wouldn't help the situation either. On the cruise, she'd returned to Krista again and again, searching for solutions. She'd opened an ebook reader on her phone, filled it with books about the environment, and read with fervor. But understanding didn't equal answers.

"It's not enough," Lacey said. He wouldn't even try, and that would never be enough. No one had answers, but somehow she had to figure out how to do something. Maybe that, the inability to accept her fate, was their difference. She wouldn't accept moving back to Texas. She never accepted subpar work from employees. Now, she couldn't accept the howl of nothingness, even if she had almost nothing to give.

The next day, she took off on her own and rode a funicular up the steep side of the fjord. The cars, reminiscent of short streetcars, perched on the side of the cliff and made their way up a rail almost parallel to the cliff. A marble balcony overlooking the entire region waited for her at the top. Sunlight sifted through the clouds and sparkled upon the water. Peace and joy should have flooded her veins at the sight, but though the landscape impressed her, an underlying anxiety thrummed through her blood.

She turned and saw a map with miles of hiking trails, picked a path, and then set off into the forest. She came across a children's park with rope zip lines, climbing walls and other attractions that looked like death traps. The children happily screamed and ran and slid, even with nothing but dirt and pinecones beneath them. She was glad of it. They'd need to be tough. Maybe she'd start a campaign to make US playgrounds more dangerous to prepare kids for a hostile world.

Dark thoughts followed her, like the trees blocking the sun above. The trail opened onto a lake, and her heart stuttered. So many beautiful places existed. This bright blue water surrounded by electric green grass and darker pines took her breath away. Some long melted glacier had likely carved the landscape. Would it burn now? Would it dry to dust? Would this happen in her lifetime? In her children's?

Lacey sat on a bench conveniently provided by whoever managed the park. Tears of despair streamed down her cheeks. How did one get beyond this if you believed the climatologists? And she believed in science. Only those who profited from it, and those who believed the profiteers' lies, didn't.

She hated herself for the constant tears and worry. Something had to give, because she couldn't tolerate another twenty years of this.

Lacey returned to the funicular and fled down the mountain and back to the apartment. Relieved to find it empty, she poured herself a glass of water and went out onto the patio. Then she called her daughter.

"Hey, Mom. Is everything okay?" Maddie sounded groggy.

Lacey looked at her phone. She hadn't remembered the time change, had acted, not thought. "I'm sorry, honey. What time is it there? I can call you back."

"No. It's almost time to get up. Give me a minute."

Lacey heard rustling, did the quick math in her head, and realized she'd called her daughter at five in the morning. "Are you sure I can't call you back at a reasonable hour?"

"This is fine, really. I'm just getting the coffee going. What's up? Are you still on the boat with dad?"

Lacey heard water running, a grinder, the clank of glass on granite. Sounds of home. The one thing she didn't have, other than a planet verging on inhospitable. She sat in one of the terrace's plastic chairs and gazed toward the harbor.

"We're off the boat and spending a few days in Bergen, as friends." It seemed important to add that last bit, not to get anyone's hopes up. "Maddie, how do you deal with the destruction the climate crisis will bring? How do you keep moving forward when it's hopeless?"

"Wow, starting with the big questions." A soft thud came through the airwaves, as if Maddie had sat down or sunk to the floor. "This is one of the biggest issues I have to deal with, that everyone I know deals with. Different people have different strategies."

"Well, I need an answer. I need something to hold on to, because I can't see a way forward." The role reversal stung Lacey to her core. She should be the one comforting her daughter, yet instead, she begged her for help.

"Start by telling me what's going on. I feel like something has changed with you."

Where should she start? Feeling useless without a job? Falling for and then getting snubbed by Sean on account of four nonbelievers from Texas? The reindeer and polar bears? Krista forcing her eyes open?

"You've been telling me about these issues for years, but here I saw the reindeer, heard about glaciers melting, realized the polar bears wouldn't make it. And I sold our family home, and the house I bought to live in burned down." Everything spewed out at once, as if she'd just vomited a confession.

"Whoa. Let's start with the last one. Your new house burned down? I don't understand." Maddie's worried voice rang in Lacey's ear.

"I think I told you I signed a contract to buy Deb's mother's place. Well, she burned it down before the sale went through, and she died."

"That's horrible. Mom, when did this happen?"

"A few days ago." Lacey sounded like she was the one with dementia. She should have contacted her daughter earlier instead of letting panic build and build.

"Mom. What is going on? Why didn't you call me? Where are you going to live? I have about a hundred other questions, including if this is why you're with Dad."

Lacey had thrown out so much information at once, she could hardly give her daughter a coherent explanation. "Your dad, well, that's something I'll explain one day, but we don't work together long term."

"No shit. I learned that one as a child."

"There's no need to get testy. I'm just becoming terribly torn up about this climate stuff. Right now, I'm looking at the gorgeous city of Bergen, and all I can do is imagine it ravaged by climate change. There's nothing I can do about it. I'm just a sixty-year-old retired woman from Carlsbad. I don't know what to do. And I feel so bad that I left this screwed up planet to you and your brother." Lacey crammed her phone between shoulder and ear and dropped her head between her legs, teetering on the edge of panic.

"Okay. Let's both take a couple of deep breaths." Maddie inhaled loudly, then Lacey heard her exhale as if she needed to shove every molecule of air from her lungs. Lacey did the same.

"There's a person I follow," Maddie said. "He says we have to plan for a better catastrophe. We've already set things in motion to raise the temperature of the planet beyond what can sustain our current civilization. That's a fact. So how do we minimize the extraordinary changes coming our way? That's one way of looking at it, and it happens to be my favorite."

"Ugh. That sounds terrible, like we're riding a ship into a burning hellhole, but a few of us have fans to mitigate the heat." If Lacey had hoped this call would cheer her up, it wouldn't. But at least the dire scenario made her anxiety real. Sean, the Texans, they didn't get it. It was as bad as she'd thought.

"What are my other options?" Lacey asked.

"Well, you can think of yourself as a soldier on a battlefield. You're completely outnumbered and you're going to lose. Take pride in the fact that you'll go down fighting."

"Maddie, that's terrible. Surely there's another option."

"You can help others. I don't mean this in a bad way, but the worst will happen after you're dead. You can work to make things better for others. Climate change isn't just about us. It started in Europe and America, then spread to countries like China and India as they industrialized. It will hurt those from poor countries in Africa, Asia, and the South Pacific the worst. Find a way to do some good in the years you have left."

Part of her wanted to chastise her daughter. She was only sixty for heaven's sake. It's not like she'd die tomorrow. But Maddie understood that. Like her mom, Maddie wasn't one to make someone feel better just because. She told the truth.

The urge to deny the harsh reality or whine that she didn't know how arose. But that's what the Texans would do. Lacey had to be different. She had to step away from internal battles and toward the war. "Part of that is what your dad thinks. He figures he'll be dead before climate change threatens Dallas."

A heavy sigh came through the phone.

"I'm sorry," Lacey said. "I'm not trying to bad-talk your dad. I just need to figure all this out."

"I know. You never said bad things about dad, and I appreciate that."

"I used to say bad things about his wife. I'm sorry about that." A twinge of guilt made Lacey say the words.

"Don't worry about it. Everyone hated her. Even the dog."

Lacey erupted into laughter. What a wonderful daughter she had. Man, she missed her kids.

"Mom, come stay with Chuck and me. We've got a futon in the extra bedroom and a pull-out sleeper in the living room. I'd really love to see you, and maybe I can help you figure this out."

"I love you too, but I couldn't impose." She said the words despite the pull on her heartstrings. She needed her daughter right now, perhaps more than her daughter had ever needed her. Lately, she'd felt like life had thrown her into the wilderness with no idea how to get herself out. But Maddie's levelheadedness and list of solutions proved she'd already traveled that path and could help Lacey find her way.

But mothers weren't supposed to rely on their daughters like that. She was supposed to lead and be the caretaker.

"It's no imposition. In fact, I insist. If it makes you feel better, you can pay rent."

Lacey laughed. How did this child always know how to lighten the mood and make things better? "Well, if you'll let me pay rent, then I might consider it."

"Mom. Get on the airplane and get your butt to San Francisco. Call me when you have your flight information."

"Yes, ma'am. See you soon. I love you."

"Where are you headed?" a voice behind her asked, startling her.

Lacey hadn't heard Sean enter the apartment. She balanced for a moment between the pull to go to Maddie's and the desire to help him to a better place. But she'd never chosen that path, whether through selfishness or self-preservation. "I'm going to stay with Maddie for a while."

"Can I come?"

Lacey turned to him, wondering whether she'd see sadness or a joke in his eyes. Their deep brown depths held a little of both.

"Let me at least get settled first," she said. She wouldn't rip away all his hope, but she had a little work to do on herself before she figured out what her future held.

Chapter 17

Lacey followed Maddie into the elevator. She'd visited her daughter before but hadn't stayed with her. Now, she planned to live with Maddie and Chuck for an indefinite, if temporary, period.

The elevator opened onto a somewhat dingy hallway with gray carpeting and white walls. She had to set new standards from the comfortable family home she'd inhabited for so many years. Just like she'd set new standards in luggage. She'd only brought a rolling suitcase and a backpack. One thing cruise life had taught her was how few clothes she really needed.

She'd spent a week at home, well, at a Carlsbad hotel, going through everything she had in storage. She'd donated clothes and furniture before she'd sold the house, but this time she attacked the chore with a ruthlessness she hadn't shown before.

She wouldn't need suits, not even the expensive ones, in her new future. So she donated them to an organization that helped women find jobs. She had far too many jackets and raincoats for a woman who lived in Southern California, even in rainy San Francisco. It would have required a separate duffle to carry them all. So most went to an organization that would distribute them to unhoused people in downtown San Diego. That donation also included blankets, sleeping bags, and a family tent they'd bought and only set up once in the backyard. She'd never enjoyed camping.

She kept furniture, art, pots and pans—things that would be useful someday. In the future, when she had her life figured out and a new place to call home.

Culling the stuff she'd tied herself to left her lighter and more ready to set off on a new adventure.

She stepped over the threshold into the apartment. A sliding glass door opened onto a small balcony, and the light brightened the small room. The space had a typical apartment setup, one long room that accommodated the living room, dining table, and kitchen. But the dark wood floors and creamy walls bright with art made the space homey.

When Maddie and Chuck first rented the space, Lacey questioned why they didn't go into a more modern building. Maddie had said they all featured gray laminated wood floors with gray walls and black and white kitchens. She promised her mother she'd be eternally depressed if she had to live in a gray apartment in a gray city.

She'd chosen well. Even though the appliances and kitchen fixtures could have been newer, Maddie and Chuck had made this place into a cozy home.

Maddie led Lacey into the small second bedroom. Stuffed with two desks and a futon sofa, it hardly had room for two people and a rolling bag.

"Chuck's going to help me move this desk into the living room," Maddie said. "I don't use it much now that I'm going back to the office every day. That will give you a little more room."

"Thanks, but I can manage. I don't want to be an imposition."

Maddie dropped to the futon and patted the seat beside her. "Sit."

Lacey recognized the look on her daughter's face. "I think I'm about to get a lecture."

"You called me a bossy little kid for a reason." Maddie smirked. "And you are going to get a lecture. Let. It. All. Go. Everything you're worried about, release it. You only have two jobs here: rest and explore."

"Well, I've just come back from a cruise. I got plenty of rest."

"Mom, you look exhausted."

Lacey certainly hadn't felt her best lately, but she'd hoped it didn't show. So much for that. "Every woman wants to hear how great they look. Thank you."

"No snark," Maddie said. "You know I'm right."

Lacey sighed. And nodded. "Yes, ma'am. What's next?"

"Explore. Walk around the city. Potrero is a great neighborhood, and there's a big park just a couple of blocks away. Wander the streets. But I want you to do more than that. I've made a list of nonprofits that accept volunteers. I'd love for you to go to all of them, but you have to go to at least three. That's your rent for staying here."

Lacey gazed into her daughter's steel blue eyes. She looked remarkably like Lacey had at that age, with dark brown hair, a small frown line running between her brows. But Maddie seemed so much more sophisticated. It also helped that she didn't have a perm or wear brightly colored eyeshadow the way Lacey had at her age. Not to mention the stupid man suits with a bow tied at the neck.

Maddie's volunteering mandate seemed like a lot, but she meant well. And it's not like Lacey had a full agenda. "You should have been a project manager with that kind of organization," Lacey said to her daughter.

"I learned from the best." Maddie reached out and wrapped her mother in a hug. "Everything's going to be okay. I promise."

Lacey fought to keep the tears at bay. She loved Maddie with her whole heart. Tears arrived quickly these days. She even cried watching a TV commercial the other day. She'd invited Deb to their regular bar, and they'd both noticed a commercial about accepting women's bodies. Out of nowhere, emotion overtook her and tears streamed down her cheeks. She looked at Deb, who matched her red eyes and tears. At least Deb had the excuse that her mother had just died.

Poor Deb. She was as lost as Lacey, maybe even more so. She'd divorced years ago. Both her kids had left for college, but her mother still tied her to San Diego. With that tether suddenly cut, Deb had nothing but her job tying her down. A job she hated more and more every day.

Unlike Lacey, Deb had gotten a big promotion. Now she worked for one of those monster women who backstabbed and put other women down. She complained her boss spent half her day sabotaging her work.

Just what the fuck were women supposed to do these days? At least if she volunteered somewhere, she could quit whenever she wanted. Not that she'd made her mind up about volunteering. She gave her daughter a sharp squeeze then backed out of the hug. "I accept your mandate. Show me your list."

"I'll email it to you. I've linked all the organizations to their websites so you can learn more about them. See if there's something out there that you really enjoy. Get involved. I promise it will help you deal with the hopelessness you're feeling."

Lacey pushed the tears down, again. "I will."

"One more thing." Maddie paused and took a deep breath before continuing. "What the hell is going on with you and Dad? And I've got to tell you, I'm kind of terrified of the answer."

"It's nothing. When Zach told him I was on a cruise in Norway, he decided to surprise me and meet me on the ship."

"That's so weird. Have you two been getting together over the years?"

"No. Never." Lacey understood how strange it would seem to her kids, but once she got over the shock, being with Sean had been the most normal thing in the world. "He's lonely, and like me, he's trying to figure out what to do with the rest of his life."

"But why you? I mean, I know you don't hate each other or anything, but why not talk to a friend?"

She considered the question and the complicated tether she had to Sean. They had started out as twin planets that had drifted apart but remained in each other's gravitational pull. "I think it's partly because of you and Zach. You've never been afraid to tell your parents how you feel about them and about the world. That is very different from what he's exposed to with his friends from Texas. Also, he and I were there for each other when we started our careers. Somehow, it's fitting that we talk to each other about winding them down and choosing our next path in life."

She wished she'd had that clarity about their relationship from the moment he'd arrived in Norway. Maybe then they could have waxed philosophically without the physical engagement. But actually, she'd enjoyed that. It warmed her just to think about it.

Lacey quickly thought about cold showers and glaciers. She hoped the color hadn't risen in her cheeks.

"Mom! You didn't sleep with him, did you? That's gross."

Lacey panicked. She didn't want to tell the truth, but her daughter always caught her in lies. Finally, she blew out a breath of air. Fuck it. Of course, that's what got her into this situation. "It's not gross. It's how we made you."

Maddie shook her head, all judgement. "No wonder you're so screwed up right now. But since you're here, we're going to fix things."

After just thirty minutes in the apartment, the first pinprick of needing to leave pierced Lacey. She might need to figure things out, but she wouldn't let her daughter do that for her. She wasn't someone's project.

"Uh, oh. There's the Mom look," Maddie said. "I think I went a little too far. I'm so glad you're here, just a little surprised about Dad. Maybe we'll work on him next." A huge, teasing grin lit her face.

"Good luck with that." Lacey stood. "Can I help you move the desk? Then I'll unpack. What time are our reservations tonight?" She'd asked Maddie to reserve a table at her favorite restaurant for Maddie and Zach and invited Zach to bring a guest. Mom's treat.

"Seven. Zach says he's not bringing anyone."

"Maybe he's our next project. I always hoped he'd settle down."

"He's fine, and don't mom up on him. He's having fun." Maddie gave her the side eye. "And don't ask me when I'm getting married or having kids. I just don't know if that's in the cards, but Chuck and I are very happy."

When I was your age reached the tip of Lacey's tongue, but she stopped herself. At her age, she didn't have to worry about bringing children into a burning planet. Well, she should have, but no one knew that back then. Back when they could have made a difference.

Chapter 18

A week later, Lacey saw Zach the minute she stepped off the Bart metro. He had his dad's dark wavy hair and broad shoulders and her blue eyes. He gave her a big hug, even though she'd seen him at dinner a few days ago.

She'd wanted to get out of Maddie and Chuck's apartment. The place was small for three people, especially on a Saturday when they'd be home all day. Plus, she'd never seen Zach's place and wanted to spend some quality time with her youngest.

"It's half a mile to my place. Are you sure you don't want to get a car?" he asked as they left the station.

"Half a mile is nothing." She'd walked all over San Francisco, just as Maddie had asked. It hadn't solved any problems, but it gave her something to do with herself during the day.

"So, you've been going through some changes recently." Zach walked slightly ahead of her, leading the way on the narrow, uneven sidewalk. He glanced back at her when he spoke. "How's it going?"

Great question, and one she wished she had a good answer to. "Honestly, I'm not sure. It's not so much retirement as coming to grips with how our world is changing. It's like I'm going through the same stages of grief I went through when my parents died. One minute I'm pissed off that we let this happen to the world, the next minute I think surely it can't be that bad, and then I usually follow it up by becoming incredibly depressed."

Zach made sharing her concerns easy. He had a sixth sense for reading people. As a boy, he'd give her a hug or rub her back whenever she verged on becoming overwhelmed with stress. He just knew, and having someone you loved show you they cared always made the moment better.

"I get it," he said. "I think that happens to all of us when we come to terms with how terrifying climate change has become. The rich feel guilty while the poor have to figure out how to survive when heat or storms come their way. And that doesn't even address how climate change may impact food security for everyone in the future."

"I shouldn't complain because there are so many people worse off than me." Lacey looked up at the old home they passed. More of a mansion than a home, it had grand wooden scrollwork and a peaked roof with slate shingles. The faded and peeling paint along with a weedy yard assured her the house had seen better days. Lacey stopped and peered through the iron fence.

"It's beautiful, isn't it?" Zach asked. "We've got some incredible older homes in this neighborhood."

"It's gorgeous here. The streets practically drip with trees, and so many people have gardens." They'd just passed a home with two lime trees and planter boxes full of cherry tomatoes. "I didn't expect Oakland to look like this."

"Oakland gets a bad rap. But this neighborhood, Piedmont, is amazing."

She had to agree. Each block brought something new, a house with an incredible succulent garden, a craftsman home with a deep porch and gorgeous stained-glass windows. Most of the houses looked well cared for, with carefully matched paint schemes and well-tended yards. Every so often, they passed a home or apartment building that needed a little love. At one of these, a three-story home that someone had divided into multiple apartments, Zach turned into the driveway.

Lacey couldn't help the pang that went through her. She wanted more for Zach than this. He led her past the main building to a granny flat in the back corner of the lot. A stone path led from the parking area to the entrance, which had a tiny porch and a powder blue door.

The inside of the flat had wood floors and an eclectic mix-mash of furniture, rugs, and artwork. When she'd gotten her first apartment in Dallas a million years ago, she'd bought matching furniture along with art and throw pillows so the place looked designed, or at least designed according to the magazines she'd read. This was much more fun.

A small bedroom to the right of the door housed a bed with no headboard. A blue velvet couch and minimalist metal and wood desk vied for space in the living area. When Zach led her through the house to the kitchen, she noticed the floor sagged. Oh, well. At least he didn't own it.

"It's really cute," she said.

"I like it, and it's easy to get to downtown Oakland where the city offices are. Unfortunately, I'll be looking for another place soon."

"Why?"

"I had a roommate, but he got a job in Santa Cruz and moved out a couple of weeks ago. The rent's too high for just one person."

"You had a roommate?" She couldn't imagine where another person would sleep in this small space. Oh—maybe it was a boyfriend roommate.

"Mom, your face is entirely transparent. See this ladder? It goes to a loft. There's another bed up there."

"Sorry." She pulled herself up the ladder to take a peek and escape her embarrassment. The room had a mattress on the floor and a small loveseat that must have had its legs removed. A bookshelf stuffed with books lined the back wall. Cute, but impossible to imagine staying there. Not with as many times as she had to get up in the middle of the night these days. She'd kill herself coming down that ladder in the dark.

She climbed back down, worrying about where her son would move next. He never asked for help, but she knew he didn't make much money, didn't have a car.

"How about I take you to brunch?" she asked.

"That sounds amazing. I can't wait to show you Piedmont Avenue."

She understood why he loved it the second they turned onto the street. Anything you needed and so many things you had no idea you wanted graced the street. They passed an old-fashioned ice cream shop that Zach promised had the best sundaes in town, a vintage theater, restaurants with windows opening onto the sidewalk. The aroma emanating from the French bakery smelled so good she stood in the doorway and inhaled. Independent bookstores sold their wares on both sides of the street. They'd walked six blocks before Lacey saw her first chain, a Peet's coffee shop. Zach led her across the street and into a different coffee shop that had a glass window full of amazing pastries and a hearty breakfast menu.

Lacey ordered a chai and a breakfast sandwich with egg and cheese on sourdough, while Zach got a black coffee and a breakfast burrito. They sat outside on a back patio, enjoying the cool but sunny morning.

"I can see why you love it here. This is a darling neighborhood."

"It's great. I've never felt so at home before."

"Not in Carlsbad?" The question slipped out before she could stop it. She'd always considered Carlsbad perfect for kids—great schools, low crime, a beach. She'd sacrificed a lot to raise them there and had asked herself more than once if they'd have been better off in Texas. The answer remained a firm no.

"Carlsbad was great. It's just, well, it's very white, wealthy, and conventional. It was fine growing up there. I just need something different now. I need to be in a place where I can make a difference."

His last sentence floored her. "You feel like you're making a difference? How? Lately I haven't felt that was possible."

He looked at her a long moment before answering. "I'm not trying to save the world or postpone disaster. That's what Maddie does. I'm trying to make things better for individuals. I find people housing, food, educational opportunities. When I can, I show them how to have their voices heard by voting, speaking at city council meetings, things like that."

"That sounds important." She hoped her voice conveyed what her mind couldn't. His efforts helped, but if no one survived, did it matter? Her thoughts spun downward, a whirlpool of despair that might drown her. A week on Maddie's program hadn't helped.

"It's important to the people I help, and that makes it important to me. I don't have any grand plan to save the world. In fact, I think it's too late for that. My vocation, my life's work, is to make life easier for the people in my city. I see so much heartache, and I get to lessen some of that. My work is profound, at least to me."

Her heart ripped in two at his words. He was a healer and a hospice worker all in one. He couldn't stop suffering, but he could ease someone's affliction. Profound was the perfect word.

"You are amazing. I'm so proud of you."

Lacey leaned back in her chair and examined her child. How had she helped create someone so compassionate? Clearly, he'd seen beyond her list making, rule-following, project worshiping self and had dug past that veneer to where the human heart existed. She had a lot to learn from him.

"You make it sound so rewarding. I've spent my life optimizing systems. What you do sounds so much more important. "

"Mom, you've done important work. You've made sure medical devices got built and forwarded to those who needed them. I'm sure you've made a difference in many people's lives, but you've never gotten to meet them. You didn't hold their hands while something worked or cried with them when it didn't. I want to be a part of those moments."

"It changes the perspective of things," Lacey said, grabbing onto an idea. "It's like staring at a looking glass from the wrong end. It's still beautiful, even if it's not what was intended."

"I like that analogy. I think we have to focus the looking glass on a human scale. We got lost when we thought everything was supposed to be on a grander scale. We're meant for the campfire, not the steamship or nuclear power plant."

She sipped her chai and let the spicy, creamy liquid warm her. The world shifted a little as she saw it through Zach's eyes. "I never knew you were such a philosopher."

"No, I'm not sure you did. Dad either. Maddie was the smart one, and I was the gay one."

He might as well have slapped her. "I don't think that's fair. Earlier today I was thinking about how good you were at reading others' emotions. You always comforted me when I was stressed. Hell, you're half the reason I even knew I was stressed. I certainly don't think being gay is your primary attribute."

"I'm sorry. I probably shouldn't have said that. It just feels like you and Dad see Maddie as the sun. The world revolves around her. What I do is important too."

So many emotions tugged at Lacey. She wanted to comfort her child, but she also wanted to acknowledge his words. Maddie was like the sun in how brightly she burned. Zach's qualities were equally important, if not so blindingly bright. She could see how he might feel lost in his sister's glare.

"If she is the sun, then you are the moon. You are my light when the world seems dark."

Lacey fought the tears that invaded her eyes. How could Zach think he was less than anyone when such wisdom and compassion flowed through his veins?

"I have been in such a horrible, dark place lately," she said. "Wracked with guilt, furious at myself and the rest of the world. Insanely angry at your dad." She shook her head, remembering the weeks of stormy emotions. "And then, over breakfast, you turn my world around by giving me a perspective I hadn't thought of. You are amazing, and don't you ever forget that."

"If you had to pick one word to describe me, what would it be?" he asked.

"Wise. Compassionate. Loving. You're the fucking second coming, kid."

His smile didn't reach his eyes, but perhaps he didn't want the tears that filled them to drop. "Thanks, Mom. I love you too."

On the way back to his apartment, they stopped in a local grocery store so Zach could pick up some fruit. Lacey couldn't ever remember visiting such an incredible store. They had homemade soups and sandwiches, bountiful produce, and local olives, oils, and cheeses. Fresh cakes and pies sat under glass, while in another section a butcher filled custom orders. Small by modern grocery standards, the alcohol section could have stocked a high-class bar.

Lacey wanted to fill a cart with staples and another with treats. She insisted on buying Zach as many groceries as he'd let her, and she purchased several boxes of tea and a local honey for herself.

Loaded down with goods, Zach led her down a side street to get back to his flat. Three houses away from the grocery, Lacey stopped. A blue Victorian home with a lush yard and two front doors had a for sale sign hanging over the fence.

Lacey didn't tell her kids when she called the real estate agent. Or when she took a car back to Piedmont to visit the house.

She met Kim at the front gate. The tall Black woman's smile welcomed her. Zach was right, Lacey had never met a Black real estate agent in Carlsbad. Maybe if she stepped out of the bubble her life had been there, she would experience a more interesting world.

Before they'd reached the front doors, Kim had asked Lacey about her life and congratulated her on her recent retirement. Kim had also divulged that she'd spent an entire career as a biomedical researcher before retiring and becoming a real estate agent.

"How do you do it?" Lacey asked. "I've been waiting for my retirement for so long that I can't imagine going back to work. I've earned this time off." The comment sounded more hollow than it used to.

"That's what I thought for the first year. My life was all travel and pedicures. Then, I got bored. I wanted to be around people. And real estate is flexible. I don't have to be at an office eight to five. I meet new people all the time, and helping folks find their next home is gratifying." Kim stepped up to the landing and opened the lockbox.

The two front doors hung next to each other on the left side of the house. Kim explained that the family home had been split into two, with the door to the left entering a stairwell to the upstairs apartment.

They started on the larger right side, where a carved door and transom window opened onto a high-ceilinged living area. Lacey noticed the original pine floors with their narrow slats and the large bay window that let in light. The window had a built-in-seating area that formed a cozy nook for reading.

Kim led her into a dining room with a beautiful chandelier, and then into the relatively small kitchen. At some point a previous owner had redone the kitchen, although not particularly well. The dark granite tile countertops didn't go with the slate floor, and the natural wood cabinets looked like they'd come from sale stock at Home Depot.

Kim must have seen her face drop. "It's functional, and you can always redo it."

Not at this price. But Lacey didn't say the words. The house would strain her budget, but if she used all the proceeds of her Carlsbad home and her retirement settlement, she could afford the house without a mortgage. She could also quit being a snob and get used to black instead of stainless appliances and a kitchen not quite as nice as in the home she'd just sold.

"It's fine," she said. "Let's see the rest of the house."

They toured the three bedrooms and two bathrooms, and Lacey learned that the door they'd come through opened to the entire downstairs portion of the two-story home. She appreciated that, because if she lived on this side, she wouldn't have to navigate stairs as she aged.

The right-hand front door opened directly onto a set of steep stairs. She climbed them and entered a large and bright dining room that connected to a raised living area. The same wood floors from downstairs graced this space, and the light blue walls and many windows made it almost feel like a treehouse.

The kitchen matched the one downstairs, only smaller, although the apartment also had two generous bedrooms and two baths. One bathroom connected to a laundry space. The owner, not a contractor, must have remodeled the bathroom, as the toilet sat askew and something about the shower seemed off.

"All of this can be fixed," Kim said, as if she'd read Lacey's thoughts.

"Except for this bathroom, and maybe the kitchen, this space is gorgeous. I can't get over the high ceilings and large bedrooms. It'd be a wonderful place to live."

"Yes, and you can use this upstairs apartment as a long-term or vacation rental. That's what the current owners have done. It would give you some income for renovations."

It was a great idea, a normal one. But Lacey already had plans for the space. She had never considered herself prone to rash decisions, at least not until she'd retired. But she'd already fallen in love with the house, and the thought of being near her children filled her heart with joy. She told Kim she wanted to make an offer. Immediately.

She hid the decision from her kids even after the owners accepted her offer, worried they'd think her decision reckless. Instead, she scheduled the inspection and negotiated what needed to be fixed with the enormity of the purchase bottled up inside her. She almost called Sean, especially when she had real estate related questions. Although he worked in commercial, not residential real estate, he had decades of knowledge.

She'd stared at her phone more than once wanting to enter his phone number. She didn't. He might tell the kids. Even if she asked him not to, she didn't trust him not to let it slip. Plus, he might judge her. She sat with that thought for a moment and realized she feared her kids' judgement, not Sean's. What if they didn't want her so close? What if Zach didn't want to live in the upstairs apartment like she'd planned?

She called Deb. Lacey needed to return to Carlsbad anyway, to get her furniture moved. Her fingers shook as she pressed Deb's photo on her phone, as if she had to get her big news out before it detonated.

"I bought a house!" She practically screeched the words.

"What? Where?" Deb asked.

"Up here in a community called Piedmont, near where Zach lives."

"Wow. The kids must be so excited."

"They don't know." Lacey whispered the words.

"What do you mean, they don't know?" Deb's confusion came across as a slurry that dulled Lacey's excitement.

"I close next week."

"What's going on? Why haven't you told them?"

Lacey paused, part of her wanting to scream through the airwaves *why can't you just be happy for me*? The bigger part of her knew she had to face her fears. "I've been so lost, and I had such a wonderful time touring Zach's neighborhood with him. It really felt like home. And then when I saw this darling home for sale, I just went for it."

"I feel like you're not telling me part of the story."

"The house is wonderful. It's got two separate living spaces. One downstairs with three bedrooms and an upstairs apartment with two bedrooms." She waited for Deb's comment, but it didn't come. "Zach told me he'd have to leave the place he's renting since his roommate moved out." Lacey couldn't go on. She'd set all this up and hadn't even asked Zach if he wanted his mom as his landlord. Or without asking Maddie if she minded her mom providing such a lavish gift to her brother.

"Oh, Honey." Deb's voice dripped with compassion. "You've got to tell them."

"I know. I think I'm out of practice with this family stuff. I've got to start being more open with them. I promise I'll talk to them."

"Listen, if it doesn't work out, I'll take the apartment." Deb's voice cracked.

"What's wrong? Are you okay?" All Lacey heard was sobbing.

"I'm just so damn lonely since Mom died. I honestly hate my life right now." The crying continued.

"I wish I were there to hug you. I'm coming down next week to deal with the furniture. Can I stay with you? We need to talk."

"Please stay with me. Stay as long as you like. I really need someone here right now."

"Okay. Let me see how quickly I can get a flight out. I'm sure Maddie and Chuck would love to have their apartment back."

After they hung up, Lacey sat in her daughter's empty apartment. Her life had been one quick change after another in the two months since she'd retired. First the cruise and then the ridiculous interlude with Sean. During that time, she'd sunk into a depression about the future, hers as well as the world's. Everything had seemed so big and overwhelming.

Despite Maddie's plan, Lacey had come no closer to figuring out the next stage of her life by walking the city streets or volunteering. But now, with her new house and her reconnection with Deb, something had shifted. She couldn't name it yet, but buying the house and reaching out to her old friend felt right.

Although she still had to tell her kids what she'd done.

She made a few texts and then a dinner reservation. Tonight, she'd tell them, then leave for Carlsbad as soon as possible to help Deb.

Chapter 19

Lacey sat at an outdoor table. An awning and overhead heaters held the cold at bay. Chuck arrived first. Tall and red-headed, he had the strong jaw of an athlete and the thick, black-framed glasses of a nerd. His looks fit him perfectly, computer geek during the week and triathlete on the weekends.

Lacey loved him with her whole heart because of the way he loved her daughter. She'd wondered if Maddie would ever find anyone to put up with her demanding personality. Her daughter pushed herself relentlessly, but she'd found her match in Chuck. Maddie became softer around him. Lacey only wished they'd make it permanent and have beautiful children together. Although she shouldn't voice those desires.

Zach arrived next, and Lacey's heart relocated to her throat, knowing what she'd have to tell him tonight. Why hadn't she brought him in earlier? Because he might say no, and she needed this for herself as much as for him. She held onto his hug a second longer than usual.

When Maddie arrived, they ordered Indonesian corn fritters, several kinds of vegetarian dumplings, and a double order of spicy noodles with tofu. Lacey kept waiting for the right moment to share her news. She thought maybe once they had their drinks, or perhaps after they ordered. Of course, the longer she waited, the harder it became.

The fritters arrived, and she reached for one. The garbanzo bean sized corn kernels dotted into the crispy patties had become a favorite treat. She broke off a piece and stuffed it in her mouth, ensuring she couldn't speak.

"Why are you acting weird?" Maddie asked, staring at her mother.

She finished chewing, then took a sip of wine, girding herself. "I have some news. I'm heading back to Carlsbad tomorrow because I need to pack. I've bought a place here."

"What?" her kids asked simultaneously.

"Where?" Maddie added.

"Actually," she looked at Zach and held his gaze. "I bought a house in Piedmont. I loved it so much when you showed me around."

Zach stared at her, eyes gone round in shock. "Really?"

Maddie broke in. "Mom, have you totally lost it? What's going on? This seems like another rash decision. Plus, houses around here are expensive. How could you afford it?"

"I am completely sane." Lacey heard the indignation in her voice. Her daughter got under her skin so easily. "And I certainly know whether or not I can afford a house. This place is gorgeous, and it's a good value. I didn't think you'd have a problem with my moving up here, but maybe I was wrong." She aimed the last question at Maddie.

"Of course we don't have a problem with it." Maddie moderated her voice and reached for Lacey's hand. "But you have to admit, that one came clear out of left field. I had no idea you wanted to live here."

"We'd love to have you in the area," Zach said. "I'm glad you chose Piedmont. It gives me one more reason to visit you."

Lacey took a breath and addressed Zach. She might as well tell them everything. "The house has been divided into two units. I know you have to move out of your current apartment. If you're interested, you can move into the smaller unit at the new house."

Zach glanced at his sister, and his cheeks went red. Had Lacey gotten it wrong? Would he not even consider living with her?

"Well, that's certainly a nice deal." Maddie's voice dripped with sarcasm.

"Maddie." Chuck said it softly, but it had an immediate effect. Maddie sat back in her chair and huffed but said nothing else.

"That's extremely generous. Um, when do you think you'll move in?" Zach asked.

"I'm not positive. I'm going to Carlsbad tomorrow night to start arranging things."

"Tomorrow night! I offer you a place to stay, do everything I can to pull you out of the doldrums you're in, and you give me less than twenty-four hours' notice that you're leaving?" Maddie's hurt voice seemed to mask a Richter scale of anger.

Lacey hadn't expected her reaction. "Honey, I so appreciate you and Chuck opening your home to me, but I've been underfoot. You two need your space back. I thought you'd be excited about my move because I'll get to spend so much more time with you kids."

Maddie huffed again. Tension swirled around the table. Then Maddie turned to her brother. "Good job, baby brother. Now you'll have a place to live, maybe free rent. That's hard to come by in the Bay Area."

"Is this going to be a problem?" Zach asked. "I'm just learning about this too."

Chuck stroked Maddie's back, but she seemed to vibrate with negative energy.

"You're acting like this is unfair," Lacey said to Maddie.

"Well, it is, kind of. I mean, you're giving him an apartment."

"Maddie, I'm disappointed in you. Yes, I am offering your brother a place to live, but what about when we paid for your graduate school? Was that fair? Your brother didn't go to grad school."

"That's because he didn't want to."

"Let's take a walk," Chuck said, rising from his seat. Maddie flashed him a look of hot fury, but she rose and followed him from the restaurant.

"Well, that's not how I expected that to go." Lacey dropped the fritter, her appetite gone.

"It was a big surprise," Zach said.

"Will you take the apartment? We can discuss any rent after you see it."

"I don't know. I haven't even seen it yet. It would help me out of a bind, but I'm almost thirty. It doesn't seem like I should move in with my parents. Let me think about it."

"You do need to see the place. I love you, and it would bring me great joy to have you live so close. You could also help me with things around the house if that makes you feel better."

"Why don't we talk more when you get back?"

Lacey nodded. "Do you mind holding down the table? I need to talk to your sister. I'll send Chuck back in here."

When Lacey stepped out into the frigid night, she didn't see Maddie or Chuck. She walked to the closest corner and looked up and down the cross street. Nothing. The fog had rolled in, creating a wet cold, and she pulled her inadequate cardigan across her chest. How could September be so chilly? She gritted her teeth, hoping she hadn't made a terrible mistake.

She re-entered the restaurant. Zach looked forlorn as he sat at the round table set for five. Lacey had tried to fix everything. She'd set out to travel the world, and the world bit her back. She'd done everything Maddie had asked but felt no closer to saving the planet, not to mention herself. And now she'd struck out and done what she thought would help her and her son the most, and that had imploded. Right now, it didn't feel like she'd survive retirement and still have relationships with her children. Not to mention her ex-husband.

She dropped into a chair, no longer hungry. "I'm not sure Maddie is coming back."

The waiter arrived, dropping a platter of sumptuous food onto the table. Zach asked him if he'd pack it to go.

Failure. The word echoed through Lacey's head. She'd been the boss for so long, and while she hadn't been promoted when she wanted it, no one had challenged her in years. At least not with anything important on the line. It had just been weeks, and she couldn't seem to do anything right.

"I'm sorry. It seems like I've screwed everything up." She could use some comfort, something Zach provided freely.

"Mom, I think you need to think about what you truly want in your life. For you. Not for the planet. Not for your kids."

The waiter arrived with a paper bag full of food. Zach stood and removed a container from the bag. "Do you mind if I take this?"

Lacey nodded. She didn't want him to leave. But she hadn't earned the right to ask him to stay.

"I love you, Mom." He gave her a kiss and a half hug.

She sat alone at the table. How ironic. In Norway, at the beginning of this unsatisfying retirement journey, she'd convinced herself to eat alone. Well, she'd achieved that, although not in the way she'd intended.

Two choices remained. She could stay at this table forever, perhaps start crying and melt into the upholstery. Or she could get up and try to fix all the things she'd broken.

She trudged to the beautiful old Westin Hotel on Union Square to catch a cab back to Maddie's. Golden light glowed from the lobby, and the people inside looked warm and happy. Nothing stopped her from walking inside, renting a room for the night, and seeing if the morning improved her outlook.

But she needed to see her daughter and at least try to understand what had upset Maddie so much. She found a taxi and sank into the back seat with her bag of once delicious smelling food. Now it turned her stomach.

The cab stole down quiet streets. Usually, the city bustled with people, but tonight, it looked abandoned. The perfect accompaniment to how she felt. She wished she had an app like the driver used to tell her where to go. Instead, she'd have to figure it out herself. No one would alert her to where the traffic snarled, when the bridge was out, or when she'd made a wrong turn. And she seemed particularly good at making wrong turns lately.

In minutes, far too fast, the cab dropped her at Maddie's. She approached the apartment door with trepidation, especially when she heard voices inside. She'd hoped to arrive first, leave the food in the kitchen, and not have to face her daughter until morning. By then, it would be too late for anger. Maddie would leave for work, and before she returned, Lacey would leave for the airport.

Lacey braced herself and used her borrowed key to open the door. Chuck and Maddie stood close in the kitchen. Upset voices reached her, louder than they should have been for two people standing shoulder to shoulder. They turned as she closed the door, their eyes like spotlights.

"Hi. I brought the food for you, if you're hungry." She walked forward, wishing she could transport herself to any other place. A Norwegian cruise ship sounded perfect. "I'm really sorry I've upset you. That wasn't my intention. I wish I understood why you're so angry."

Lacey saw a flame light in Maddie at her mother's words. Fire licked her cheeks red, and an angry glow reflected in her eyes. An eruption was coming.

"What's happened to you? Growing up, you were always so reliable. Boring maybe, but reliable. And now, it's like you're completely unmoored. Floating off to Norway, getting together with Dad, and now buying a house, two houses, without telling anyone. I don't even know you anymore."

"You do know me." Lacey thought for a moment. "Or maybe you don't. The only me you've ever known worked full-time. That woman had to be highly organized, regimented even, just to get through the day because she was busy raising two kids and making money. Money that helped pay your expenses growing up. Money that sent you to college and grad school. Money that means that after working like a dog my whole life, I can retire and not have to live with my kids, although somehow, I ended up doing that despite all my planning."

She paused, hoping her words would sink in. The look on Maddie's face didn't change. Lacey couldn't tell if her daughter would dress her down or leave the room next.

To prevent those options, she kept talking. "You know what? No one gives you a guide for the right way to retire. And it's not like I did no research. I did. You wouldn't believe how many cruises I've looked into. I thought that would be my future. But instead, on the very first one, I kept hearing about climate change. I saw it. I saw how it affected people and animals and ecosystems. And that brought on a fucking ton of guilt."

Lacey couldn't stand still. Her words spiraled into a tornado of energy, forcing her to pace back and forth in the small space. Every muscle tensed, and it seemed like all the blood rushed to her head, setting off a massive headache.

"And then what was I supposed to do? More research! This time on the impact of cruises on climate change. And it's terrible. Well, I already feel guilty about leaving this shit show of a planet to my kids—a planet I helped to pollute. My generation got all the benefits of burning fossil fuels. We got cars at sixteen, traveled the world, reveled in the computer age. And all of that stuff poisoned the planet. But not while I'm alive. Instead, it's going to wait until my children and grandchildren must pay for how I've lived. And it sucks. And I'm pissed off. And I don't know what to do about it. But I promise you, I'm doing the very best I can."

Finally, she talked herself out. She stood, energy zinging through her body, but she made herself stand still and prepared herself for Maddie's response. Chuck raised his hand to Maddie's back, probably to comfort her. Hopefully not to encourage her.

"I have been trying to help you," Maddie said, as frustration and anger slammed across the room. "I knew you were struggling. I could hear it in your voice. And that thing with Dad told me you were in bad shape. So I tried to help. When you didn't have a place to go, I invited you here. When you were lost and feeling guilty about the climate, which believe me, I go through on a daily basis, I put together a plan to help you. I've been there for you, and then you go and buy a whole house without even letting me know. Relationships are a two-way street—at least for most people."

"Thank you for inviting me into your home. I appreciate everything you've done for me. But I am not required to check in with you when I decide to buy a house. I had a contract on a place in Carlsbad. Unfortunately, it burned down, leaving me without a home. I didn't run that purchase by you, and you didn't seem to mind. Do you not want me here?"

"You asked for my help. If you're going to do that, you need to check in with me. If you don't, how can I help you?"

"I'm not your child. I'm a grown woman, and I can do whatever I want with my money. And with my life."

"But you asked for help!"

"You offered, so I came to see you. I wasn't handing my life over for you to manage." Had she? She remembered the loss that had gone through her, the dark place she'd entered when she'd felt like she'd done everything wrong in her entire life and then she'd lost the security of home. And she'd placed a desperate phone call to Maddie from Bergen. Maybe she had leaned too hard on her daughter. But that didn't mean she wanted to give up her autonomy. Not when she'd finally earned it after so many decades of reporting to others.

The tension between the two women threatened to burst the small kitchen into flames. Lacey could acquiesce, but some core of who she used to be, the tough businessperson who rammed projects through on time and on budget, tightened.

Lacey studied Maddie carefully. Her daughter's nostrils flared, reminding her of a bull about to run down a matador. The anger of her daughter pulled at her to take her in her arms, pat her head, and make her feel better. But first she'd save herself. Just like in a crashing airplane, she needed to put her own mask on first.

"I'm sorry I've upset you. I can see it was a mistake to come here, and I'll be gone tomorrow. Whatever's wrong between us needs to be fixed, and I commit to working on that. But not today." Her words wouldn't make anything better, but at least she'd set some boundaries.

"I just want my mom back." Maddie's voice shook with passion.

Her words slapped Lacey. She hadn't changed. Well, she had. Her life circumstances had changed, and that necessitated a new attitude or way of looking at things. And shouldn't learning new things make you grow? Surely, she had taught her daughter that.

"I love you, honey, and I wish you weren't angry with me." Lacey sighed, giving up. "I'll be out of your hair tomorrow."

She retreated to the tiny extra bedroom her daughter had so generously shared, although it came with strings she hadn't seen. She pulled her suitcase onto the bed and carefully placed one item after another into the interior.

It took every ounce of strength to remain calm, to fold the clothes precisely. She wanted to rip each item in two. Or light them on fire. Or throw them into the chaos of her brain which would destroy them completely.

She used to be someone. Her hands shook as she folded a T-shirt. Once, not so long ago, she'd had a place where she belonged. And a family who loved her. She grabbed the edge of the suitcase and sank to the futon.

She longed to walk into her office, where people would say hello or want to discuss a project they both understood. Her heart longed to return to a world where she hadn't disappointed her children but could pick up the phone and their voices would bring her joy.

Retirement had brought her freedom, but she hadn't known the cost. Belonging. And somehow, she'd squandered the belonging of family, along with most of her money, on a house in a place she barely knew.

Some lost emotion wanted to shove the suitcase to the floor, lie on the futon, and cry until she fell asleep. That kind of healing tirade also seemed lost to her, perhaps lost to youth along with smooth skin and a bright future. She placed a pair of socks in the suitcase.

At least she still had Deb. She'd return to Carlsbad, to sunshine and warm air. Maybe she'd check in with Michele from work and see how things were going. Her kids still loved her, but she needed people who liked her, with whom conversations weren't battles. Hopefully, those chats would return some stability to her world. She was going to need it.

Chapter 20

Lacey did not want to drive past Deb's Mom's burned down house. Her once imagined post-retirement respite.

"But I go there almost every day," Deb said. "I sit in the yard, look at the condo and cry."

"Why do you do that to yourself?" Talk about self-flagellation.

"Well, it depends. Sometimes I'm sad that Mom left so suddenly, even though I realize her life with dementia would have been terrible. Other times, like when I hear from the insurance company or contractors, I cry because this may break me financially. Mom didn't have enough insurance on her place."

"You're kidding," Lacey said. Deb always seemed to get the brunt of a bad situation. Unlike Lacey's relatively amicable divorce, Deb's husband had cheated on her and spent most of their money. Fortunately, he couldn't touch the kids' college savings accounts, but the divorce left Deb in a financial hole. Now she faced additional money issues with her mom's house.

"It's been awful, although it's mostly taken care of now. The kitchen is a complete loss and there's a lot of smoke damage, but I've found a contractor to put everything back together again who is way cheaper than the one the insurance company recommended."

"And you're sure he's good? I don't want you to get swindled again. Not after what your mom ended up paying for the remodel." Lacey wished Deb had asked for help. Making good decisions became difficult when emotions overwhelmed practicality. Lacey knew that one personally.

"Believe me, I've checked reviews, references, and interviewed multiple contractors. The one I'm going with came highly recommended, and she's a woman."

"That's fantastic. Instead of visiting your mom's place, why don't we go down to the sea-wall for a walk?"

Thankfully, Deb acquiesced. Lacey had to leave the past behind. She wanted a bright future so badly, she just needed to stop screwing up. Deb turned the car toward the ocean.

They found a parking space in a lot overlooking the Pacific. The teal water breaking into frothy waves settled her. How beautiful this world was.

She thought back to the water in Norway, a colder, darker sea, but perhaps the world's swirling currents mixed drops from that ocean with the water here, a connected, ever-changing mass.

They stepped out of the car and headed toward the water. A few steps in, Lacey noticed the stench. "What is that?"

Deb waved her hand in front of her face. "I forgot. There's a red tide right now."

"Again? We just had one last spring." Lacey hated it when warming ocean water caused algae blooms that choked the ocean, killing sea lions and dolphins and causing a gut-wrenching stink. Climate change comes home.

"Let's go somewhere else," Deb said, turning around. Lacey gave a wistful look at the sea she loved, then followed her friend.

Deb turned on the engine, but Lacey put a hand on her arm. "Wait. Let's talk for a moment. And the whole sordid story spewed from her. Buying a house on a whim, pissing off both her children. Sleeping with her ex-husband. Learning about the world she'd helped set aflame. Missing the community of work. It all floated together in a stew of unhappiness. But somewhere deep inside her, hope remained.

She finished her story and saw a tear trickling down Deb's cheek. For a brief second, she thought it was sympathy, then realization slammed into her. Deb had experienced something a thousand times worse over the same weeks.

"I wish I had a house in Piedmont. I'd give anything to be somewhere else. My kids aren't even here anymore and now that you've left, I'm so fucking lonely. What happened to me? I used to have so many friends."

"Me too," Lacey said. "When the kids were in school, I had so many women friends. But we lost touch after they graduated. Some people moved away, others stayed involved in school activities with younger kids. Even my book club fell apart. I'm not even sure why. Did I just get too busy?"

"It's such a bummer. Maybe once I redo Mom's house, I'll look for a job up near you. After all, Cory's in school at Santa Cruz. That's not so far away." Deb grabbed a tissue from the console and patted under her eyes. "I have got to stop crying. Every day, I cry. You'd think I'd be out of tears by now."

Lacey squeezed her friend's hand. "Never run out of tears. They show you care."

The women stared out of the windshield, watching surfers seated on their boards waiting for the perfect wave, despite the state of the water. The rhythmic thump of crashing water sounded in her ears and beat in her chest. She loved the ocean.

Her thoughts slowed to match time with the waves. She loved the water in front of her and the land beneath her feet. Well, maybe not the parking lot, but the sand and the grass and the trees. Thoughts of immense red sequoias filled her mind. The magical grandfathers and grandmothers of the forest had watched over the land for centuries. The life of a squirrel, a deer, a person, was nothing to them.

Lacey used to take the kids there for spring break. Hiking among the mighty trees of the eastern Sierra might have sparked Maddie's love of nature. And now a changing climate threatened those giants. The ranger explained how their range could shift over millennia, but not fast enough to avoid killing temperatures, heat-adapted insects, and increased fire. But she loved them still.

She loved her children. Her choice of a home had sparked a conflagration, yet they would get beyond it. She might not have enough love to heal the world, but she had enough to heal their rift.

She loved Deb. She and this best of friends had survived marriages falling apart, children, and careers together. This, she would hold on to.

"Move in with me," Lacey said.

Deb looked at her, eyebrows raised. "I was just whining. I'll be fine. Really."

"I'm serious. You have nothing to hold you here but a job. With your project management skills, you should be able to get a job anywhere. Especially in the Bay Area. And the house is plenty big. I've got three bedrooms and two baths and only need one of each."

She'd made the offer on a whim, but it made so much sense. Her house had room. Deb could have her own bed and bath and there would still be an extra bedroom. And there would be a built-in friend for as long as Deb wanted to stay. That sounded infinitely better than hundreds of strangers on a boat.

"But you wanted Zach to move in."

"There's a whole separate apartment for him. Please." She clasped her hands in prayer. "I'm so fucking lonely too. I need you. You'd be close to one of your kids. The other's in Santa Cruz, not too far away. At least consider it."

Deb laughed, looking suddenly ten years younger. "I'll consider it."

Lacey wished she could make all her friend's burdens vanish. "If you move in with me, you can sell your house here, and as soon as it's fixed, you can sell your mom's house. Heck, you might even be able to retire."

"I don't think that's in the cards. At least not until Cory's done with college." Deb inhaled deeply, then seemed to release half her tension in the exhale. "It would be nice not to have to worry about money all the time."

"I even know of a couple of project management jobs that I found during my search."

"You are an angel," Deb said.

Lacey couldn't hide her smile. A single root of brightness tapped into the soil of her heart. Maybe the answer wasn't to save everything. Maybe it was to save what you could while building something beautiful, a community of good people filled with love.

Her heart brimmed. From hopelessness to heartfulness. Was this something she could aspire to? It felt right. The blue house in Piedmont could be her base in the world, the center of her heart. She'd fill it with people she loved, good work, and hope for the future. Surely, she could make this work.

A week later, Lacey returned to the Bay Area. She rented a small flat in Piedmont for a week. Then she'd move into her new house. The furniture would arrive the day after she closed.

She'd texted her kids several times. She let them know she both wanted to make Piedmont her home, and she wanted strong relationships with them. As soon as she rented the flat, she gave them her plan and texted them the address. No more hiding things. Zach's responses had been short: "I understand" and "Thanks." Maddie's had been nonexistent.

It worried her. While Lacey shared some blame for their argument, Maddie had overreacted. Lacey figured deeper forces drove the dramatic response, and she hoped to learn what and why.

All this she figured out on her trip from Carlsbad to Piedmont. She broke up the long drive by spending the night in Three Rivers, just outside Sequoia National Park. In the morning, she drove through that and the adjacent Kings Canyon National Park. She wanted to stop and place her hands on a giant Sequoia. She couldn't look at the massive trees without understanding how ancient they were. History ran through each ring, along with sunlight and storms, and quiet nights that blessed the red bark.

She stopped in one of the many parking areas and made her way to an enormous tree. Its crown rose over two-hundred feet above her, and its humongous trunk had to be twenty feet around. She laid a palm on its thick bark and tried to pour her gratitude into it. Not caring how ridiculous she appeared, she hugged the massive tree and apologized for all her species had done wrong.

Even now, as she pulled into the narrow parking spot at her rental, she felt the sequoia's bark against her palms. She had naively thought she could change things, but perhaps bearing witness to the wonders of the earth was the important thing, the thing she could do.

She could also build a community. She needed connection with others to grow older. She'd thought retirement meant a life of leisure on one's own, but what a horrible existence that would be. Even the cruise wouldn't have been as much fun without Sean.

She would start over with an open heart. She would build something new, the way she'd once built a career. Hopefully, she would connect with others. Deb, Krista from the boat, who lived with her mother close by in the Berkeley Hills. Her children. Her heart pressed hard at that one, driving her to rush to their homes, love them, and demand they love her back. But those relationships would come in time, when they were ready.

She made her way from the apartment to the car to unload more luggage. As she turned to trot back up the steps, waiting on the stoop stood Sean. It shocked her to see him.

"What are you doing here?" Had he come because he loved her? Because he couldn't get her out of his mind after their fling? She shook her head. Why did her mind always go there first, like a little girl searching for her one true love?

"I wanted to see how you were doing."

"What does that mean?"

"Are you going to invite me in?"

"I don't know yet." She wanted to open him up like a papaya and read the black seeds inside to divine his true intentions.

"Please, Lacey. Let's talk."

And in her heart of hearts, she still loved him. As a friend. And the father of her children. A memory of his skin against hers, hot and sweaty, in the small bed on the big boat. Stop. She couldn't go down that road. Not without getting flushed. Or showing him the bed in the apartment. Weren't these feelings supposed to end post-menopause? Obviously not.

A lanky young man with a beard came out the front door. "Good morning," he said before striding across the lawn.

"Yes, I guess you better come inside." Better that than maintain this awkward standoff.

Sean followed her up a set of stairs and to a room at the back of the house. She noticed a stain on the carpet near the window. A tinge of embarrassment lit her skin. Here she was, sixty years old, and living in an apartment like a teenager. She shoved those feelings away. What did she care what he thought?

"Welcome to my home sweet home. For a week anyway." She saw the one-bedroom apartment through his eyes. A tiny kitchenette along one wall, a table for two with plastic chairs, the least expensive gray sofa from the furniture store. But it was clean, and the many windows let in lots of light, and she was an adult god damn it. She got to live her own life.

"Oh, Lacey." The judgement in his voice twisted her with humiliation.

She spun around. "Why are you really here?"

"The kids are worried about you."

"Why? Because I get to live my own life and make my own decisions without checking in with anyone? I'm not your problem. I'm not their problem either." Hadn't she just thought about the importance of community, about rebuilding the relationship with her kids? She still didn't understand what she'd done to upset everyone so much.

"You have to admit you've been acting rash lately. You sold the house the second you retired without even thinking about it. And I know you planned to buy the condo in Carlsbad, but after that fell through, well. . ."

Thank god he wasn't stupid enough to say she'd been acting crazy. It was hard enough to keep her indignation bottled inside. She wanted to let it burst all over this tiny apartment. Instead, she dropped the bag she'd brought in. The one with the new sheets because she didn't like the ones here.

"Come on. Let's go get a coffee." She held the door open for him, assuring he'd leave.

The closest coffee shop was the one she'd visited with Zach on her first day in Piedmont. She approached the warm wooden counter and was greeted with a "welcome back," by the nice man at the cash register.

They took their coffees to the back patio. Inside the shop, the tables sat too close together to have the conversation they needed to have. And Lacey just might start yelling at her ex. No need to scare anyone, she planned to be a regular here.

"I get to choose where I live and what I do with my life, the same as you." They might as well get this over with. She'd calmed down some, but he needed to understand this wasn't a negotiation.

"Of course you do. You're just moving super fast, and the kids are worried." He used his calming voice, the one she hated the most.

"I found a home I absolutely love in a place that's close to my children. I don't understand how this is a red flag for anyone." There. That should put him in his place.

"But you hid it from your kids. Why not involve them?"

"Because it's my decision." And because she didn't want them to tell her no.

Sean looked at her as if he'd heard the words she didn't say.

"I'm worried about you too. One minute you're talking about spending the rest of your life on cruise ships, and the next you decide to save the world. And you were pretty rude to the people I introduced you to on the boat."

"They were assholes."

Sean cocked an eyebrow at her but said nothing. At least he wouldn't debate that point, and it gave her time to put the rest of her thoughts in order. They needed order.

"I think I had a dream that during retirement, I could make up for how hard I worked during my life. Being a single mom, even with your generous financial support, was hard. Clawing my way up the ladder was difficult and incredibly frustrating. When I got the buyout, I wanted to kick up my feet and relax for the rest of my days."

Lacey sat back in her chair and took a long sip of coffee. The idea of retirement differed from how she actually wanted to spend the rest of her life. Why had that taken so long to click into place?

"You deserve that," Sean said.

"Yeah." She did deserve it. "But that's not really what I want. I needed that trip to Norway. It gave me the time and space to think about the future. I don't want to spend my life gallivanting about the world, not being useful to anyone. A life like that doesn't have meaning. And you meet too many assholes."

"So now you want to save the world? You said you've worked hard your whole life and you're just going to throw yourself back out there." Sean ran a hand through his hair. "That's it? You just toil until you die?"

He'd asked the last question for himself, not for her. He'd asked it for himself and for everyone else their age who had to figure out the next twenty to thirty years.

"I don't think it's toil when you find the right focus. And I don't think I'm going to save the world. It's already too far gone for that."

"What the fuck does that mean?" His anger surprised her.

"I've done some research, and I've listened to the people Maddie sent me to volunteer with. Last summer we surpassed 1.5 degrees Celsius, the increase the papers all told us we needed to stop at to avoid a global crisis. Despite this, governments around the globe have done nothing to truly mitigate climate change. In some ways, it's out of our hands now."

He mussed his hair again. Seeing him frustrated and vulnerable, her heart shifted. This was how they needed to be there for each other. When the truth finally sank into someone's heart, they needed a friend who cared. Just like when you lost a loved one. The suffering happened on one's own, like Deb continually returning to her mother's burned house. But having someone who understood your pain and trauma helped.

"We have to come together to mourn for our planet. And we need to do what we can to make it the best crisis it can be."

"This doesn't even make sense. We've talked about this. I probably won't personally see any impact from climate change."

"Just because it's not on your doorstep doesn't mean it's not happening. And things in Texas are worse, people are just afraid to admit it's climate change. Also, we can't close our eyes to what we're doing to the rest of the world." Lacey worked to keep her voice calm, while Sean tensed like a cat about to leap across a chasm.

"I know what's happening in the rest of the world. It's not like I do nothing. I recycle. I give money. How have you changed your life to make a difference? By traipsing all over the world and deciding to buy houses right and left?"

"That's not fair." Well, the house comment wasn't fair. But what had she done to make a difference? Hugged a redwood? Change had to be both systemic and individual. She knew that from project management.

"Not enough. I need to do more individually. Maybe I'll quit flying or get rid of my car or plant a garden. Maybe all of them. I also would love to find an organization I can contribute to that works on broader, more systemic change." The tasks in front of her seemed impossible to surmount. "It's difficult to know where to start."

At her softer voice, he seemed to calm. Some of the fight had gone out of both of them.

"So, why did you decide to start with a house? And why didn't you tell the kids?"

Lacey sighed. She didn't know all the reasons, but she knew enough to be honest with him. She grinned at him, this man who'd colored her life for so many years. They were just trying to find a way forward.

"I bought the house because I truly loved it from the moment I saw it. I think I didn't tell the kids because I didn't want them to tell me no. I love our daughter, but she can be super bossy. Living with her wasn't a good idea."

"Yeah, I see how that would be problematic. You know, she's just like you."

"That's probably why we butt heads. Although, she seems more easily upset than usual. Are you staying with her?"

"Me? No way. I'm staying at the Westin."

"Of course you are. Come. Let's take a walk."

She led him back through the coffee shop and across the street. They passed the local grocery where she'd shop from now on. Joy pulled her toward the house, but she experienced a tight apprehension as well. What if this was like the apartment earlier? She'd thought it was fine until she saw it through his eyes. Some small part of her feared she'd made a mistake.

She stopped in front of the wooden fence, its gate topped by a lattice arch. The blue house with its two front doors and Victorian scrollwork practically smiled back at her.

"This is it," she said.

Lacey glanced at Sean while he studied the house. She wanted to rip his thoughts from his mind, force them out of his lips.

"It's darling," he said. "You did good."

"Thank you." She threw herself into his arms, relieved, proud, and glad he remained a friend.

Chapter 21

Lacey slid into the wooden booth of the Thai restaurant, and Zach followed to sit beside her. Sean had suggested they all meet for dinner before he left town. Maddie had bowed out, telling her father she didn't feel well.

"So, what's up with your sister?" Lacey asked. "She won't even have dinner with me?" She tried to sound casual, but it didn't work.

"She said she was feeling a little under the weather and didn't want to get anyone else sick." Sean's comment from across the table prickled at her. Lacey ignored him and kept her focus on Zach.

"She's been uptight the last couple of months. Maybe something's going on at work," Zach offered.

Lacey had dealt with work stress her whole life but had worked hard to keep it out of the rest of her life. Maddie had a similar disposition. Something particular about the purchase of this house had set her off.

"That wouldn't explain what infuriated her when I told you about the house. Has she said anything to you about not wanting me in San Francisco?"

Sean looked like he wanted to jump into the conversation, so Lacey sent him a sharp glance. One good thing about having lived with someone for years meant you knew how to shut them down.

"I think it was just a surprise." Zach picked up the menu, turned it over, and then set it back down. "Plus, she called me the next day and told me it wasn't fair that you'd bought a place for me."

"What?" The comment enraged Lacey. "Why on earth would she think that?"

"Housing is expensive in the Bay Area. She feels like she got the short end of the stick."

"We paid for her graduate school. You never went. Although, if you wanted to, we'd help." Anger raced through Lacey. What an ungrateful little snot her daughter had become. And to blame her sweet son instead of talking to her about it made her fume.

"I think Maddie just needs a cooling off period." Sean said, diplomatic now that he'd avoided the middle of his children's disputes for once. Lacey wanted to tell him to stay out of it, but most of all, her fingers itched to slap some sense into her daughter. Not literally, but Maddie needed a come to momma meeting.

"Zach, have you considered your mother's offer? I saw the house today and, at least from the outside, it's pretty cute."

Lacey crossed her fingers, hoping for a positive response. And she had to admit, Sean changing the direction of the conversation had taken the tension down a notch. Sometimes she wished things had been different between them. But it hadn't worked out that way, and he'd fly back to Dallas in the morning. They'd kept the relationship platonic during this visit, but the chemistry lingered.

Zach blew out a heavy sigh. "It would be fantastic, particularly if I could rent it at below market rates, at least until I found a roommate. But it also makes me feel like a loser. I never wanted to be that kid who moved back into his parents' house as an adult."

A waitress came by, and Lacey shook her head at the woman. They could order after she'd dealt with Zach. She reached out and took one of his hands in both of hers. "It would mean a lot to me if you lived in the apartment, for a couple of reasons. First, I am really proud of what you're doing with your life, how you bring community members together to make positive change happen, but it's not something that's going to make you much money. Cheaper rent could be my contribution to this effort. We're going to need people looking after each other in the coming years. That you're spending your life doing this should be celebrated and financed. Second, I'm lonely. I don't expect you to solve that. I'll make friends here. In fact, I'm meeting with someone I met on the cruise tomorrow." She'd tell him about how Krista had convinced her to join a sit-in at the Wells Fargo Bank headquarters after Sean had left.

Finally, she said, "Having you close—it would mean the world to me."

"Thanks, Mom." He squeezed her fingers, and happiness spilled through her. She could pull this off. She could build a community of people she loved one step at a time. Maddie was a missing cornerstone, but she'd find a way to remedy that. She just needed to keep building, brick by brick.

"You've really thought this out." Sean's voice didn't carry its usual heft. Lacey recognized the sound of loneliness that had walked beside her for longer than she'd realized.

"You know, if Dallas doesn't work out for you, you're always welcome here." Not in her house, maybe, but nearby.

"Thanks. Both younger boys are still in Texas, so I'll stay there for now. I wish I could clone myself and be in two places."

Yeah. He'd have chosen that path a long time ago if he could have. But she'd never wanted a clone of a man. Maybe someday she'd find a man to share her life with, hopefully someone like Sean, but someone who could fully commit to a life without wanting to spend half of it elsewhere.

She felt sorry for him, because he always missed out on half his life. She wouldn't do that. Instead, she'd build her community and find a way to contribute like her son and daughter and Krista. And she'd create a life she could love for the end of her days and the end of the world. Something bloomed in her heart at the idea. Love. A new kind of love, one with roots in a whole community. Could she avoid the mistakes of the past as she moved forward? Lacey couldn't see that far ahead, yet she had hope.

Krista met her at the BART station so they could take the train to downtown San Francisco together. Lacey had packed a picnic basket stocked with treats from the local grocery store, including a fabulous looking banana bread, caprese sandwiches, and kettle chips. She also threw in two cans of grapefruit soda and water bottles.

Krista waited for her on the platform. She held two tall cylindrical bags, one hunter green, the other charcoal.

"These are our rocking chairs," Krista said.

"Rocking chairs?"

"Yep. You're now part of the rocking chair rebellion." Krista raised her hand for a high five.

"Okay?" Lacey's palm met Krista's, but she didn't share her enthusiasm. It made her sound like an old fogey.

The train came, and they boarded, scoring seats together in the post rush hour traffic. Soon they sped alongside the freeway, before turning and dipping down under the bay. She loved the Bay Area Transit System, something so much better than anything she'd had in Carlsbad or Texas.

They got off downtown and walked a few short blocks to the bank's headquarters. Krista had explained how the big US banks financed the fossil fuel companies. Her group had started out protesting oil companies, but they had no incentive to give up their main business. In fact, petroleum companies like Exxon and Chevron had lied about the true impacts of climate change for decades, spreading misinformation and lobbying at every level of government.

"It makes more sense to go after the banks that fund them. Fossil fuel companies are only about five percent of the bank's customers."

"Yeah. I'm a customer, although my net worth is nothing compared to Exxon," Lacey said.

"You should change to a bank that promotes climate justice and doesn't invest in fossil fuels," Krista said. "There are plenty of resources on the Third Act website."

"My son has been telling me that for years. He gave me a recommendation. I think it's time to act on that. Is Third Act the nonprofit that organized the sit in?" Lacey asked.

"Yes, I think you'll love it. I do. I've made some wonderful friends in the group. It's easy because you have to be sixty or older to join."

"So, it's all old people?" Lacey asked.

Krista laughed. "Do you consider yourself old?"

"Only when I look in the mirror." It still surprised her sometimes, those wrinkles that had threatened for years now suddenly trenched into her forehead. Not to mention the no longer taut jawline. But she didn't feel old. She never thought of herself as old mentally, and that hadn't changed since her twenties or thirties.

"Same," Krista said. "It's a young at heart group, although age-wise, you'll certainly be one of the younger ones."

That sounded fantastic. Lacey had an August birthday, and she'd always been one of the youngest in her school classes. She hit the workforce early and climbed the corporate ladder quickly, at least until she stalled out the last ten years of her career. She hadn't been the young one in any group for a while.

They turned the corner and saw the protest. The bank had cement planters on the sidewalk as if to protect its fancy glass façade. Scrollwork above the door announced Wells Fargo and Company. The thirty or so protesters kept the sidewalk's main pathway clear, but they'd set up their rockers among the planters. Lacey and Krista joined them, placing their chairs at one end of the demonstration. Not everyone had chairs. Some people stood in small groups, talking and laughing as if this were a football tailgate or backyard party instead of a protest. Many had signs supporting climate change and calling for the divestment of fossil fuels.

"This may be more fun than I expected," Lacey said. The people looked friendly, and excitement flowed through the cool air.

"It could get dicey if we decide to occupy the lobby." A tall man on the other side of Krista spoke. "Hi. I'm Gus."

Krista stepped back and Lacey got a full view of Gus. At over six feet tall, with sinewy muscles and olive skin, he looked her age, and incredibly vibrant. Desire flashed through her gut. If guys like this came to protests, she'd come every time.

"Gus, this is my friend Lacey. This is her first protest."

"Welcome. We're glad to have you here. You haven't been through our training yet, so you might want to stay on the sidelines when we occupy the lobby. There's a possibility some of our group will be arrested."

"Arrested!" That was the last thing she'd expected.

"Yes. The police arrested seventy people at the Citibank protest in New York earlier this year."

"What for? I thought these were peaceful protests." Gus was hot and all, but she didn't want to share a jail cell with him.

"We're trying to create change," Gus said. "We are peaceful, but sometimes the other side isn't. Think of the Civil Rights Movement or more recent protests. I believe it's better that we get arrested than have our kids and grandkids thrown in jail. The cops are nicer to gray-hairs, especially white ones."

"And how do they treat you, Gustavo Ortiz?" Krista asked.

"The gray hair provides plenty of protection."

Lacey noticed that his hair contained at least as much pepper as salt. And he had dreamy mahogany eyes. She gave her head a shake. Honestly, how could she be daydreaming about this guy? She'd come here to work.

"Are you all right?" Gus asked.

"Absolutely. I've got my rocker and I'm ready to roll." OMG. Spoken like a true dork. Fortunately, Gus and Krista laughed.

The group of protesters started filtering over, eager to meet the new arrivals. Lacey met four women friends wearing orange signs around their necks affixed with photos of their grandchildren. Grandchildren seemed to drive many of the protesters, although Lacey met more than a few who shared her guilt about the way she'd lived her life. Lacey had expected to be the only one who'd come to this type of volunteerism so late. Instead, she fit right in, just another person struggling to make sense of the world.

Soon, the crowd broke into song. Never a talented singer, Lacey rocked and hummed along. No standing and clapping for her. Gus also stood on the sidelines for the songs.

He served as the natural leader of the group when a couple of police officers came by. He approached them, and after a short conversation, they went on their way. Lacey gave a smile of appreciation, and he nodded back at her.

About an hour into the event, he approached the guard standing at the bank's entrance and told him something. Then, he returned to the group and made an announcement. They would occupy the lobby in fifteen minutes. Someone passed around sheets of colored paper with *Divest from Oil & Gas* printed on them.

A thrill ran through Lacey. She'd always followed the rules, kept her nose clean. That she'd do something that could get her thrown in jail would have seemed impossible even a few months ago. Now, it might happen. Excitement beat out fear, in part because she had a new group of friends who'd be right there with her.

Gus approached. "If you're not comfortable with this, you can stay out here."

"Actually, I really appreciate what you said earlier about peaceful protests. This is important work." Retiring, going on a cruise, certainly purchasing her new home, had brought her personal thrills. But this might make a difference in the world. She wondered if Maddie would be proud of her, or if it would add to her anger. Either way, she was going to grab hold of this newfound purpose.

Before they had the chance to enter the lobby, the security guard entered the building. Then someone came and locked the front door.

Lacey ran up to Gus. "What are they doing? They're ruining it."

He laughed. "Slow down there. We made our point and forced them to close the lobby. That's not cheap for them. If we keep pinching them hard enough, they'll move."

Lacey couldn't hold back her newfound energy. "I really wanted to wreak a little havoc."

Gus shook his head, his brown eyes sparkling. "We did all right for one day. Remember, this won't be a quick fight."

"It hadn't occurred to me before, but it makes sense now. If we want to create change, we've got to put ourselves on the line. And as a white, CIS woman of a certain age, I probably don't have much to worry about."

"You've always got to stay alert, but it's harder than you think to get arrested. Even if you do, peaceful protesting usually won't get you much more than a few hours in jail. Climate change is the real violence. It destroys lives and steals the future."

Lacey wanted that kind of passion in her life. "I'm glad we've got a fearless leader to follow." She stared directly into his eyes as she said it so he wouldn't miss the point.

"Oh, there are plenty of things I'm afraid of. If you agree to have a drink with me tonight, I'll tell you a few of them."

She smiled so big it made her cheeks hurt. "That sounds great. Although, I live over in Piedmont." Traffic in this city could kill a person, and who knows what part of the megalopolis he called home.

"Fantastic. I'm in Oakland. Let me get your phone number."

They exchanged numbers and plans. He'd pick her up at her place at eight and they'd head for the Lakeside Lounge for a couple of drinks. Best day ever—except maybe for the singing.

She wandered back to Krista and the other rockers. Krista gave her a sly smile when she sat back down.

"Seems you've been spending a little time with Gus," Krista teased.

"He's pretty cute. Anything I should know about him?"

"Nothing that I'm aware of. He seems like a nice guy, taught at one of the community colleges, and yeah, pretty cute. I think he plays the field a little."

"That makes him even more attractive," Lacey quipped.

They started packing to return home. "How often do you do this?" Lacey asked.

"We've only done it a few times since I joined. I think we should do it more often. Anything we can do to keep pressure on the banks."

"Count me in anytime."

"Will do. And you ought to change your bank. Listen to your kids. They sound smart."

"I'll get to work on that this afternoon." She forced her voice to be cheerful, but she'd have to fix her relationship with Maddie to be truly happy or at least get her to return her calls and texts.

Still, the rest of it she could do. How hard could changing one's bank be? The people at the protest had given her other tips. She could buy less stuff, eat less meat, buy local. She'd heard the same things from her kids for years, but something about hearing it from her peers made a difference. Heaven knows, she had enough jeans and yoga pants to last the rest of her life. She could fly less, or not at all. Grow food—an entire lifetime of possibilities waited for her.

Plus. She had a date tonight. A budding confidence took root. She'd experienced many new things since retiring. It reminded her of going off to college for the first time or getting married, as the circumstances of her life changed, she changed as well. The push and pull of exciting new changes and the wanting to settle down and build something permanent kept her on edge. It fascinated her to wonder what tonight and tomorrow would bring.

Chapter 22

Lacey slid on her darkest pair of jeans and a gray sweater with a little sparkle running through the weave. Cranberry lipstick and black mascara called out her best features. She didn't want to try too hard, although she kind of did. Falling into bed with Sean had smacked of destiny by accident, but this was a proper date.

Would waiting outside look too desperate? She did it anyway. No need to buzz him inside to see her shabby apartment. She took one more look in the mirror. *You've got this.*

Gus arrived right on time. He pulled to the curb in an older silver Honda Accord, not exactly the vehicle she'd expected. He looked like a man's man, all broad shoulders and five o'clock shadow. In Texas, that would have meant a pickup truck, in Carlsbad, perhaps a fancy electric vehicle. But his big smile welcomed her as she slid into the front seat.

"You look fantastic," he said, and the scrape of his eyes across her skin told her he meant it.

"You look pretty good yourself." Red plaid shirt over a black tee, faded jeans—he had a rugged look, far different from the corporate America she'd dated in the past.

The fifteen-minute drive wound through hilly Piedmont, then crossed the freeway to flatter ground. Soon, they circled a small lake.

"I didn't realize Oakland had an actual lake," Lacey said.

"You live in the nice part of town. Once you cross the freeway, you're in Oakland proper, although it's gentrified plenty over the years. The city has spent tons of money redeveloping the lakeshore. By the way, the Lakeside Lounge isn't actually on the lake."

Sure enough, they turned away from the water and a few blocks later pulled up to a red brick storefront squeezed between two larger buildings. The words *Lakeside Lounge* sprawled across a cheery blue and white awning.

"You know," Gus said, not moving to get out of the car. "We can go to a fancier place, one that's really on the lake. This place is like a second home to me, but it definitely puts the dive in dive bar."

Lacey laughed. "I misspent half my youth in a dive bar in Texas called the Long Branch. This looks like a step up." She flashed him her biggest smile and opened the car door.

When Gus pushed through the door to the bar, sound buffeted Lacey. *Bitches Brew,* one of her favorite jazz albums. She stepped inside with confidence, only to have it shrink from her the minute she saw the crowd. She'd heard about Oakland's diversity. Black and brown women and men looked happy and at home. She was the only white person in the bar. This would never happen at the Long Branch.

She chalked it up to another learning experience. The world looked like this, not like some Dallas suburb. She turned to Gus. "Where do you want to sit?"

"It's pretty crowded already, but I see a couple of seats at the bar. If a table opens up, we'll grab it." Gus took her hand and led her forward.

"Hi, Angie. How's it going tonight?" he said to the stunning woman behind the bar. She had to be in her forties or fifties with a short afro and a body that wouldn't stop. She wore what looked like the bad girl version of the Sandra Dee outfit.

"It's hoppin'. What'll you have? We have a special on Singapore Slings."

"I'll have a Bud. Lacey, what would you like?"

She definitely didn't want a Bud. "I'll try the Singapore Sling."

Cowed by the gorgeous bartender, she didn't ask what the drink contained. Hopefully, she'd like it. She glanced around the room, and a warm glow settled into her as she studied the people. Everyone had a few years on them. She didn't see anyone in their twenties or thirties, and plenty of people had reached her age or more.

"I think this is my new favorite bar," she said, leaning into Gus so he could hear her over the voices and music.

"Why is that?" He settled a warm hand on her back as he leaned in as well.

"No Teenie-boppers."

"True, and they've got spectacular music. A band will play later tonight."

"That sounds wonderful." She looked into his smoldering eyes, already wanting to kiss him. That thing that had happened on the boat with Sean had reawakened something voluptuous and feminine inside her. She longed to fan that flame. She bit her bottom lip, trying to keep the feeling inside. After all, she hardly knew him.

"Here are your drinks." Angie plopped a beer can and a bright red cocktail onto the counter and slid them forward.

The spell broken, Lacey picked up the beverage and took a sip. The drink might look like red Kool-Aid, but wow, it packed a punch. It also tasted far better than Kool-Aid. She caught pineapple, cherry, and probably gin. A lot of gin.

"How is it?" Gus asked.

"I think I'm going to be a cheap date tonight, but it's delicious."

"Yeah, they're known for their strong drinks. I'll make sure you get home okay."

I'll bet. She hoped he'd take very good care of her tonight. She pulled her mind out of the bedroom. "How did you get involved with the protest?"

"I'm a long-time environmentalist. I like pressing for big change, like divestment. But I also try to make an individual difference. That old car we came in, that was Honda's first plug-in hybrid."

"Oh. That's pretty cool. I drive a Prius."

"Not bad. What got you involved in the movement?"

"My kids mostly. One's an environmental attorney and the other works in the city's housing program."

"Here in Oakland? That's pretty cool. My kids are here too. One's an electrician like his dad and my daughter is raising her two kids."

A red flag popped into Lacey's head. "You're single, right?"

He grinned but suddenly looked much sadder. "Yes. I lost my wife to cancer when the kids were young."

"I'm so sorry." What a tragedy. But it gave them one thing in common. "I thought it was hard enough to raise kids on my own after a divorce. Your situation sounds incredibly tough."

"Those kids, they gave me a reason to go on. That's part of why I'm so concerned about our planet. My kids grew up hiking and camping in Redwood country, and out at Lassen and Pinnacles national parks. I want their kids to have the same opportunities."

But they won't, will they? She could think it, but not say it. How did you keep something so dire from bleeding into everything you thought, everything you were? She wanted to build a community, but if they couldn't save the world, did it matter? It had to. Something had to. Even if it was just this one night.

"I don't think my kids will have kids. It's such a shame that they'll miss out on that happiness. They're terrified of leaving them an unlivable planet. I get it. Sometimes I wish I didn't. Life would be so much easier if I could deny any of this was happening."

Gus looked at her and cocked his head sideways, as if searching for a different view. "That's true, but I choose to see this as an opportunity. Before I became aware of this crisis, I went about my days living a normal, late-twentieth century American life. I didn't have to risk my life to put food on the table or fight sabertoothed tigers to get to work. I didn't care so deeply about the planet that it almost cracked me in two. I didn't understand that each seed is a miracle, each drop of rain a portent of life or death. I sleep-walked through my life."

The words stirred something familiar in her. The daily grind—getting through days on the edge of exhaustion just to get up and have to do it all again the next morning. Wondering where all this work would get you. Could it buy you anything as valuable as the decades you'd put into it? Doubtful.

"And now?" she asked.

"After I learned how short life could be, I had to enter the battle. I am David flinging rocks at the goliath of corporate America, and I have to win."

He wrapped a large hand around his can of beer, as if considering flinging it into the fight. "My life is so much more important now. It has meaning. Humans were meant to have meaning in their lives. I used to be like everyone else, but now, the desperation I carry for this planet and every creature on it has turned my heart into something feral."

He rested a hand on her shoulder, warming the angora and pressing it into her skin. His words, the protest, inspired her. Her own feral heart stirred.

She'd almost smothered it with all the things she was supposed to do. But her buyout offer from work had cut her loose from decades of clocking in, striving for a company that would never love her back, living by society's rules. She wanted to embrace her wilder self, not spend the rest of her years on a cruise. She wanted to fight the wrongs of the world with teeth and claws, and love with them as well. She wanted to claim victory over an angry world.

A shiver of anticipation ran through her. "I hope I'm not being too forward, but when we finish our drinks, can we find someplace more private to go?" Her voice had dropped to husky. Weeks ago, she'd never have uttered such brazen words. She'd never again waste a moment of time due to convention. Niceties didn't matter while the world burned. Love, connection, making a difference—these instincts would drive her now.

He raised one eyebrow at her question. "We can go back to my place."

Lacey drained her drink.

The next morning, Lacey woke before Gus. The gray light of early morning filtered through the blinds. She scooted up in the bed, careful not to wake the man beside her, and sat up against the headboard. The king-sized bed filled most of the room. She hadn't noticed the quality of the thick cotton sheets last night when her attention had focused on his brown skin against her pale, his lean muscle hard to her soft. Now, she pulled them up to cover her bare breasts, nipples gone hard at the memories.

She slipped out of bed, pulling his soft black T-shirt over her bare skin. The morning required coffee. She padded through the bungalow, striving for silence. The kitchen looked out onto a backyard filled with raised garden beds and fruit trees. She imagined the front yard of her new home looking the same. Perhaps he could show her how.

She found the coffee maker and filled it with water. A bag of beans sat on the counter next to a grinder. She debated a moment before the pull of caffeine had her pouring the beans noisily into the grinder and pushing the button.

"Come back to bed." His sleepy voice came in like a breeze from the bedroom.

"I'll be right there." She finished the coffee, then turned the button on. It would be ready whenever they were. She laid a hand atop the cheerful mint-colored tiles that had to be original to the home, then bent over and drank straight from the faucet. She rinsed her mouth and returned to the bedroom.

"Good morning," she said. And he did look good in the morning light, all sleepy eyes and warm skin.

As she approached, he opened the covers for her. Just that gracious motion, and the sight of him naked and ready had her aching for more. She climbed on top of him, her skin lighting up where it touched his heat. He slipped his hands under the shirt, and she bent to kiss him.

Sometime later, they drank the coffee. She asked about the garden, and he gave her a tour. He grew everything: squash, tomatoes, herbs. He had two apple trees, two hazelnuts, and a pear. If the world burned down, one could start again in this Eden. She vowed to do the same.

She wanted to tell him she wasn't looking for a relationship and didn't want to tie him down. He represented a taste of freedom. Not the freedom she'd dreamed she'd have when she retired, but a freedom one grabbed when one could. She looked into his eyes and started to say something. His look told her he understood, so she kissed him instead and asked him to take her home.

He dropped her at the curb of her building, and she took his head in her hands and kissed him with all the passion he'd opened inside her. She wanted to start a gratitude journal and draw a picture of him.

"Thank you," she said. "You are wonderful." She'd never again wait to expose her true feelings.

"You're welcome. Right back at you."

She exited the car and waved as he drove away.

"Jeez, Lacey. The whole neighborhood saw that."

She spun around to see Sean standing on the porch. A wave of heat scorched through her, some from the embarrassment of getting caught, some likely a residue of the previous eight hours.

"I thought you went back to Dallas."

"I decided to stay another day. I wanted to talk to you. Who the hell was that?"

"A friend, and none of your business." She trotted up the stairs, glad she'd showered at Gus's house.

"Can we go get a coffee?" Sean asked, his voice almost pleading.

"Sure. Let's go now." She turned again and headed back to the street.

He waited a second, and when she looked back, she caught him glancing between her and the front door of her apartment. Then he followed.

They walked toward the coffee shop, but when they got to Piedmont Avenue, Lacey turned left instead of right.

"Where are you headed?" Sean asked.

"I'm ravenous, and I've been dying to try a cute diner on the street. You game?"

"Sure," he said, not sounding happy.

A teenager seated them at the window and dropped plastic menus on the table. Lacey inhaled the intoxicating aroma of sugar wafting over from the donut display. She perused the menu containing all the greasy spoon favorites. The teen came back with coffee and a paper order pad. Old school.

"I'll have the eggs, hashbrowns, bacon, and sourdough," she told the young woman. "Wait. Hold the bacon."

"I'll have what she's having, but I'm good with the bacon."

Once they'd ordered, Sean looked out at the street, seemingly lost in his thoughts. He could normally talk anyone's ear off, and his silence worried her.

"Tell me what's going on." She laid her hand atop his, hoping the comfort would help him find the words.

"What if you're wrong?"

"About last night?" Her generosity faded at his words.

"No. You get to do whatever you want regarding men. He's a lucky guy."

"He's a friend. So are you." A bold statement. But she desired to establish her place in the world. She belonged only to herself but would give freely to others. The philosophy fit as comfortably as her angora sweater.

"What if you're wrong about climate change? When I bring this stuff up with people I know back home, they've got all sorts of facts and figures about why humans didn't cause global warming, or how we'll be able to solve it with technology. What if you've upended your life for nothing?"

She pondered his words. Outside, a bright blue sky shone down upon people walking dogs, laughing with friends, an unhoused man on a street corner. How could someone believe the world had entered a period of chaotic change when everything looked the same?

She had to have faith, not in a god, but in a plethora of scientists who assured her of the truth behind the data. Yes, she'd experienced hot summers and read about bigger, more damaging hurricanes, species destruction, strained resources. But she could no more see those things than see the Holy Ghost land upon her shoulder.

"I can think of three answers to your question." She laced her fingers in his, a habit from long ago. His returned squeeze settled her.

"First, I believe in science. I believe there were dinosaurs, even though I've only seen bones, and someone could have made those out of paper mâché. I believe Earth has an atmosphere and the oceans have currents, even though I can't exactly touch them. The science is overwhelming."

The teenager came back with Melamine plates piled with food. Lacey grabbed her fork and dug into the eggs, raising a finger to ask Sean to wait. She chewed the perfectly cooked scramble, then took a forkful of hashbrowns. Dark crust, salty, and deliciously buttery, the food reminded her of how much joy one could still have in a dying world.

She took a long sip of coffee before continuing, enjoying the bitterness on her tongue. "Second, I love it here. I'm making friends, and I'm so excited about moving into the house I can hardly stand it. This place," she waved her hands toward the window, "I was meant to be here. If I'd gone back to Carlsbad, to a retirement village, no less, I'd never have experienced this excitement about the future. It would be bingo at eleven, chair yoga at two, and dinner at four. I want more from my life, and I'm going to get it here. Earlier today, I saw the most beautiful garden with raised beds. I want that at my new house. It can be a haven for me and the kids and my new friends. I want to build deep roots here, deep enough to withstand the coming crisis. If there's no crisis, living that way will still be a joy."

She plunged her fork back into her food. Sean's fingers steepled as his food grew cold. His eyes peered at her, but she had no confidence he'd listened. Aah. The question, in the end, hadn't been about her at all.

"Most importantly," she said. "What if I'm right?"

He sighed, picked up a piece of bacon. He'd cleaned his plate before he spoke again.

"I just don't know," he said. His internal struggle came through in the glint of his eyes and the muscle that twitched on his jaw.

"What if you don't know for sure, but you pretend like it's happening anyway?"

The server came back and asked if they'd like anything else. "More coffee," Lacey said. "And a plain donut."

As soon as the woman left, Lacey fixed Sean with a stare. He met her gaze but then seemed to shrink back in his chair.

"I guess that's the question. If climate change is real, then I have to figure out what I should do with my life. Do I go buy a tract of land in Washington state and take to the hills like the Unabomber? I mean, no one ever taught me how to grow my own food or whittle furniture.”

“I don't think you whittle furniture. That's for toys and stuff.”

“Well, there you go. I'm not cut out for this. And what do I tell my boys? They're far more likely to win *Love Island* than *Survivor*.”

“This—what you're doing right now is how you start. It's not easy to figure out. And yes, I've also thought about buying some land somewhere safe, if there is anywhere safe, just to give the kids and any kids they have the best chance possible at making it. But if I do that, it means I've given up.”

“And you think not ordering the bacon is going to make a difference?” She heard the frustration in his voice but hated the low blow.

“I'm still learning about all of this, but the thing that seems most certain is that fossil fuels and the industries that rely on them are doomed. Big agriculture is doomed to change or die, although they try to convince us otherwise.” She looked at him, nicely dressed in a button down and slacks, hair neatly trimmed. He belonged in an office and should play to his strengths. “In a way, you're right about bacon. Don't get me wrong, we should do everything we can to keep the looming disaster from getting worse. But the movement needs lots of things, like lobbying to force the banks to divest from funding new fossil fuel development and to get governments to fund alternative energy instead of oil. You could make a difference in Texas.”

He chuckled. “I'm afraid you overestimate my influence in state politics.”

“Well, if this thing is happening, and I think deep down you know it is, then you have to choose. Do you want to spend the rest of your life whittling furniture or twisting arms in the state capital? Hell, start at Dallas City Hall if that's what it takes. Join a group, like I did. There are already people working on this stuff.”

“What group did you join?”

“It's called Third Act. I even went to a demonstration yesterday, and some of them thought they might get arrested.” Yesterday she'd worried about that. Today, it sounded daring.

Sean raised an eyebrow, but before he could comment, the teenager set a donut in front of them. Lacey cut it in half with a knife and pushed half toward Sean. She took a big bite and moaned as the sugar and dough dissolved on her tongue. Sean's eyes went big at the sound. She smiled at him. After all, she'd moaned like that in his arms not too long ago.

Sean shook his head. "You are so distracting. Remind me to buy you donuts instead of roses if we ever start dating again. Not that I'd come visit you in jail. Getting arrested sounds pretty radical."

"Basically, the philosophy is that they're unlikely to hurt a bunch of geriatrics. We protested outside of Wells Fargo so they'd divest from fossil fuels."

"Did it work?" He picked up the donut, downing half of his half in one bite.

"Don't be an ass. You don't show up once and get everything you want. You know that. It's like trying to convince you climate change is real, and you need to do something about it. This is the fight for the rest of our lives."

"Do you actually think you've got it right this time? A few weeks ago, you spoke about spending the rest of your life on a cruise ship." His remark cut. And she deserved it.

"I was wrong. Vacations are boring. Trying to save the world is exhilarating."

"That vacation was not boring."

She bit her lip to keep from smiling, but the memories of Sean naked beside her on the ship and of last night with Gus ran like a movie through her head. She just might turn into a slutty old lady. Imagine days filled with protests, gardening, and sex.

"Believe me, protesting climate change doesn't have to be boring either. You should try it sometime."

He chuckled once, shook his head again. "Who have you turned into?"

"Exactly who I'm supposed to be."

Lacey's self-satisfaction lasted most of the way back to her apartment. They turned off the main street and ambled along the front of a stucco church. Sunshine warmed her back and the purple, red, and yellow leaves of the changing trees left her grateful for this cozy neighborhood.

"You know," Sean said. "You talked about building community but aren't you forcing your children into this definition of community?"

She stopped, as if walking and considering his words couldn't happen simultaneously. "Forcing?" It sounded evil, the opposite of her intent.

"You did move into their community. And you totally gave up the community you spent years building in Carlsbad." He'd stopped at her shoulder.

Something inside her trembled and threatened to break open. "I didn't have a community in Carlsbad, other than Deb, who I'm trying to get to move up here. I never realized that if I let all the friendships I made when the kids were young slip away, that I couldn't get them back again. For years, I turned my focus to my job and let those friends fade into the background. The only community I had was at work, and that's not mine anymore."

Lacey pressed her hands into her thighs. The tremble had moved outward, affecting her fingers and voice.

"Hey, it's okay." Sean wrapped an arm around her and pulled her into him. "I feel the same way. Getting divorced probably cut my number of friends by three quarters. I still have all the old friends from school, but now we have set times we get together. The Texas-A&M game, skeet shooting in the summer. Just stupid stuff we do because of tradition. But Dallas is the only community I know. That's why I'm worried about you."

"Well, I'm fine, so you just go on back to Texas." She grounded her voice, her spine, her feet. She would not cry in front of this man, would not regret the decisions she'd made. Lacey stepped out from under his arm and put her hands on her hips, elbows out like a prickly cactus.

"Lacey, come on." He used the soothing tone she used to hate so much.

"I've got some shopping to do while I'm out. It's been good seeing you, Sean. I hope you have a good flight back." Lacey spun and walked back toward Piedmont Avenue.

"Lacey, don't be like this."

She'd heard him utter those words so many times before. He'd chastised her for not wanting to follow him back to Texas, when he'd had to convince her to move to California in the first place. She'd made a go of it, and he hadn't. How had that become her burden?

At Piedmont, she didn't turn down the hill to the grocery store. Instead, she turned up, walking block after block, trying to get her mind to settle. Although temporarily furious with Sean, some of what he'd said held truth.

Had she just busted in on her kid's lives without asking them? Without even telling them her plans? Yes. She hadn't asked for their opinions because she didn't want to be told no. If she'd asked and they'd said no, she could have come anyway. It would have been more honest.

Piedmont Avenue ended at a grand entryway with a sweeping cut stone wall and wrought iron gates. Acres of headstones and a row of mausoleums climbed the hills on the far side of the gate. She might as well walk among the dead. She'd probably be there soon enough anyway.

Lacey strolled the peaceful rolling hills, trying to hold on to her anger with claws and teeth. Must the day be so bright and cheerful? Couldn't the cemetery be something out of a Stephen King novel like the one in Norway instead of manicured lawns and beautiful flowers?

Unlike then, today, death didn't seem a threat. It didn't seem close at all. She had years ahead of her. Piedmont was her home. She felt that in her bones.

Meaning she'd have to deal with the truths Sean had laid at her feet. On the cruise, she'd not only realized the full meaning of climate change, she'd stared into the depths of her own loneliness. She could keep it at bay with sex. A ridiculously fun, if not long-term solution. And she could more honestly build friendship and family.

Lacey finally stopped and rested on a wooden bench. This high up the hill, the view encompassed all of Oakland and the bay beyond. She could see San Francisco and the green mountains behind it that eventually led to the Pacific Ocean. She loved her new life, and she missed her old one.

She never thought she'd miss work, and she didn't miss the day-to-day, nor did she miss her managers. But she craved making decisions and being useful. Her urge to contribute went beyond having a garden and showing up at the occasional protest. She had so much more to give.

She might be getting up there in years, but she was as mentally sharp and probably as physically strong as at any point in her sixty years. Perhaps she had been collecting people to ease her into retirement, her children first and foremost. Even Deb, although she truly believed her friend needed a change to get beyond her mother's death.

Should she go back to work? The mere thought of it brought storm clouds to the bright day. She didn't want to work all day every day, with only scraps of time on evenings and weekends. But when she'd gone to meetings and volunteered, as per Maddie's directions, that had felt like sitting through boring meetings at work. She'd listened to other people reporting on what they'd done with very little true discussion about what was needed or how to utilize the volunteers at the table. It could have been an email.

Lacey had always hated meetings, unless she'd controlled the agenda. Her favorites came at the beginning of new projects when she explained the importance of their work and how each person could contribute. Her excitement infused others, and the meetings always broke with the rah-rah good intentions of a pregame motivational speech.

Her second favorite work activity involved following a project's details, to make sure each person did their part to ensure overall success. When she noticed a blip in the project plan, she could address it immediately. She often thought of herself as a cowboy or sheepdog, corralling the people and their assignments until they'd delivered the final project. Could she do just that? Not deal with HR or department budgets or any of the everyday office stuff she found tedious?

Could she do it part time? Might she be able to negotiate her future? She liked a few of the organizations Maddie had sent her to, but the way they'd wanted her to volunteer, passing out flyers or organizing meetings, wouldn't stop climate change. But if someone gave her a project. . .

She practically ran back to the apartment. When she opened the door, she wished for Sean. She'd love to tell him she figured it out. Of course she'd told him that before, a couple of times, and she hadn't quite been right. The same thing might happen again, but if she kept trying things, she'd get there. In fact, didn't the term climate change signify that the coming disaster would be a time for change, constantly reassessing the need to go in this direction or that to address the vagaries of the weather, not to mention politics and human nature?

Her plan had issues. It would take a lot to update her resume. After spending decades at the same company, she doubted she could even find her resume. Screw it. She pulled out the business cards she'd collected at the various meetings she attended. After looking up the executive director or CEO of each nonprofit, she emailed that person, telling them briefly about her experience and project management expertise and telling them she'd like to give back by managing any projects they had. She sent Gus a similar email—although she made that one a little more personal.

She had no doubt she'd eventually find the right job to give her days more meaning. Lacey hadn't wanted to think about returning to work, because somehow that seemed like failing to retire. But perhaps part of her feral heart included her Type A personality. And it was far better to create her own future than to rely on her children to make her happy. Not when they had their own lives to live.

Chapter 23

Lacey smoothed the dirt in the container's bottom, then rose to get a bag of compost. Filling the four raised garden beds she'd bought at a local nursery had turned into hard manual labor. She'd purchased the extra tall ones which stood three feet high, to make planting and picking far easier, especially as she aged.

She'd watched a YouTube video on filling the beds, and while she didn't have tree stumps to build up the lowest level, she figured she could use firewood. She'd had a load of woodchips delivered and bought topsoil and compost. Plus seeds. In her first year of gardening, she'd have the most expensive vegetables on the planet.

Lacey had originally planned on lining the entire front yard with raised beds. The amount of work required had checked her ambition. She wouldn't feed the planet on just four beds, or her community, but she'd supplement her own diet. And she'd learn, then plant more next year. She'd grown herbs and tomatoes over the years but never had anything close to a subsistence plot.

She'd just thrown the second log into the bottom of the next bed when Gus stopped by. He'd called to ask her out two nights earlier, and she opted to have him over for dinner and to see her new home. She made stir fry with noodles and bought a bottle of sake from the local market. Then they'd made love on the king-sized bed in her high-ceilinged room.

They didn't see each other regularly. She'd always loved the term friends with benefits. Her relationship with Gus focused on the benefits, which suited her fine. Lacey preferred the freedom to explore rather than be tied down.

"Hello," she said as he made his way through the gate. She felt the heat rise in her cheeks as the sight of his broad shoulders and lean waist reminded her of the way he fit beneath her when they made love. She'd never tamed a wild stallion, but he'd probably been pretty close.

"You know, when you blush like that, it makes me want to take you inside." His husky voice crossed her skin like a loofah.

"That can be arranged."

"How about I help you fill these beds first?" He removed his flannel shirt, leaving the black tee beneath it. After that maneuver, she longed to lead him to the bedroom, but she knew better than to turn down physical help in the garden.

They worked together, filling each bed until they'd used all the wood. She only had one shovel for the wood chips, so Gus started on that while she went to get them water.

She returned carrying a pitcher of ice water and two glasses. Gus had stopped working and instead talked to two young men just inside the gate. One she saw clearly, a Black man with impressive braids pulled back behind his neck.

"Hello," she called out. When Gus turned to look at her, she realized the other man was Zach. "Zach. Welcome." She'd invited him the day after the furniture arrived, but he'd texted that he was busy. Maddie hadn't bothered to respond to the invitation. Lacey left the pitcher and glasses on a small café table.

"Hi, Mom. I just stopped by to see how you were doing."

"Mom?" Gus said. "You must be Zach." He reached out to shake his hand.

"And you are?" Zach asked accusingly.

"Zach, this is Gus. He's a friend of mine." A moment of tension bounced between them. Zach likely knew what "friend" meant, and Lacey couldn't tell how he processed the news.

"It's great to see you honey," she said, slicing through the awkwardness with a hug. Then she turned her brightest smile on the man with her son. "Hi. I'm Lacey Carmichael. Zach's mom."

"Nice to meet you. I'm Isaac." He looked uncomfortable, like she might choose to hug him also.

Instead, she offered her hand. "Welcome. It's nice to meet you too."

Next, she put a hand on Gus's shoulder. "I lucked out today when Gus stopped by. He insisted on helping me fill these huge garden beds. We were just going to stop for water. Can I offer you some?"

"Actually, I was hoping to get a look at the apartment, that's if your offer still stands."

"Absolutely. Let me grab the keys." She ran up the front steps and pulled the key from a hook just inside the door. Hope welled in her that he'd like it. She wondered about Zach's relationship with Isaac. Roommate? Boyfriend? She wouldn't ask. Just like she wouldn't want to share the details of her relationship with Gus, something too new to have explainable details.

She opened the door to the upstairs apartment. "I'll let you two explore. Let me know what you think."

She returned to the table and sank into a chair. "Gus, come get some water."

He rinsed his hands with the hose and wiped them on his jeans. She appreciated the ease of this man who never seemed out of place.

"You're welcome to wash up in the bathroom." Lacey handed him a glass of water.

"Maybe later. I've still got some work to do out here. Handsome boy."

"I can't thank you enough for your help. And yes, I think Zach is wildly handsome, and I love him so much my heart almost stops when I see him. I really hope he'll decide to move into the apartment."

"I bet he will. This is a wonderful house, and from the look on his face when you introduced me, he loves you as much as you love him."

Lacey chuckled. "I think seeing you surprised him."

"Yeah. He probably thought I was the help. That's happened before." He said the words with a sly grin on his face.

"Oh, you are so much more than the help. But we don't need to tell my son that."

Just then, Zach and Isaac came out of the apartment. Zach practically leapt down the stairs. "That place is fantastic."

"I hoped you'd like it. The back bathroom is a little wonky, but we can get that fixed." She looked up at her quaint blue home with its big windows and happy demeanor. "I love this place. It feels like home."

"You know," Zach said. "I've got some extra time right now. Why don't I help you fill the beds?"

"I'd love that," Lacey said. "But I've only got one shovel."

"I bet that won't be a problem. I saw the next-door neighbor working outside when we walked up. Give me a minute."

Soon Zach returned with a shovel, a rake, and a bald, bespectacled man in tow. "I'm Clay Davis," the man said. "Your son told me you just moved in."

Lacey made introductions all the way around. Astonishingly, all the men stayed to help, and they filled the garden beds over the next forty-five minutes.

Despite the help, Lacey's muscles held a heavy tiredness that would turn sore by morning. But the ecstasy of soreness resulting in something she could touch, something that would feed her, meant far more than walking out of a sweaty gym class.

As the men threw out empty bags and straightened the yard, she retired to the kitchen for gin, tonic, ice, and limes. She brought those out on a tray with six glasses before refilling the water pitcher they'd drunk dry.

Her garden table only had two chairs, so Gus, Zach, and Isaac sat on the porch steps. Lacey pulled her chair close to her son.

"I can't thank you all enough for the help today. It would have taken me all week to finish that project."

"Mom, you've said that like ten times. It was fun, and we were glad to help."

Isaac nodded at the statement. Gus smiled and raised his eyebrows in a way that made her think of the bedroom.

"I'm happy to buy you all dinner," she said. "We can get something delivered."

"I can't stay, but I'm glad to meet you," said Clay. "If you ever need anything, I'm right next door."

"Isaac and I have a friend's birthday party tonight," Zach said. He took Isaac's hand in his. Lacey's heart warmed. "Do you mind if I stop by tomorrow so we can talk about rent?"

She hoped her grin lit up the afternoon the way his words lit her heart. "I'd love that, but you'll have to come before noon or after two. I've got an interview tomorrow."

"I've got work," he said. "But I can stop by after that, say between five-thirty and six. Now, tell me about this interview? Is it a job interview?"

"Kind of." Lacey wished she could tamp down on her pride a little, but damn, it pleased her so much to have taken this step. Someone at a company she'd reached out to had called her back for a phone interview. The man she spoke with seemed impressed with her background and invited her to the office. "I applied for a job with the Land Institute. They're implementing citizen gardens throughout the Bay Area and need a project manager."

"That's amazing," Zach said. "Right up your alley, although I'm surprised. I thought this was your first garden attempt." He gestured toward the garden beds.

"It practically is. Luckily, they have experts for that. My role would be purely project management—you know, making sure the right people are connecting, the contracts are all signed, and the right materials make it to the right places on time."

"Congratulations," Isaac said.

"Thanks. In fact, I've had a couple of other interviews as well. But I like this job and this organization the best." She did, mostly because the person who interviewed her and who would be her boss was her age. In Carlsbad, her bosses were forced upon her, but now she got to choose where to spend her time and with whom to spend it.

"I had no idea you wanted to go back to work. Is it for the money?" Zach asked, worry in his voice.

"No, it's not for the money. In fact, I plan to donate my time, and I'll only work twenty hours a week. I just need to get out there and do something positive. Plus, I think I'll enjoy working when I don't have to depend on it for my livelihood."

She wanted to say more, to mention how Maddie had inspired her and led her to this second chance to contribute. The loss of her daughter clawed at her, causing her to pick up the phone a dozen times to force a resolution. But Zach had asked her to wait, said Maddie would reach out when she was ready. And Lacey quelled her take charge nature by scrolling through photos of her daughter instead, waiting for the day they'd fix their rift.

"I'm done with the power imbalance of corporate America," Lacey said, turning her thoughts from her aching heart.

"Here, here." Zach raised a fist in salute. Gus slow clapped. Lacey basked in their approval.

"We better get going," Zach said to Isaac. "I'm definitely going to need a shower before the party." Soon, they left, walking down the street to Zach's apartment. Lacey loved that no one needed a car around here. She'd even begun thinking about selling the Prius.

Gus's warm hand met the small of her back, and she turned to him. "You know, I stopped by to ask if you wanted to go back to the Lakeside Lounge for a drink tonight." His rough voice rolled over her, making her want more than a drink.

"Thank you. Normally I'd say that sounds lovely, but I'm a little tired from all the work today. I was thinking of having a shower and then ordering in dinner. Care to join me?"

His kiss confirmed his intent. In that moment, Lacey's world felt close to perfect, except for the one missing piece of her heart.

Chapter 24

Lacey put on an extra layer of fleece before heading outside to check the garden. She'd found an extra robust blend of Colombian coffee, and she wrapped her hands around a mug as she surveyed the yard.

She'd planted crucifers, flowers, and hearty herbs. After the new year, she'd buy two more beds and expand the variety of crops in the spring. Even on a day like today, when the fog hung low and the air seemed half water, she wanted to start the day in her cozy yard.

Kale shot frilly leaves toward the sky, as if to embrace the cold, wet day. Soon, Lacey would begin her Saturday routine: a walk, a small breakfast, then maybe read a book under a warm blanket.

Saturdays used to feel like a prize for surviving the week, although a loaded one, since she had a never-ending list of chores. Before that it had been the hustle of kids sports and activities that often left her more exhausted on Sunday night than any other. Now, life had slowed nicely.

It rarely took more than two days a week to complete her tasks at work. They'd asked if they could pay her as her assignments filled a vacant position. Lacey had carefully only applied for paid, not volunteer positions to ensure jobs with real responsibilities. She talked her boss into using the funds to hire a young person who she could train to take over her work. Not that she expected to leave anytime soon.

The job had an unexpected bonus. Her boss had taken her on a date. In her old working life, she couldn't have considered this option. But since she worked for free, he didn't have undue influence over her. It might be a mistake anyway, but she doubted it. She could rely on her experience to keep her out of too much trouble.

She still saw Gus from time to time. Years ago, her fling with the guy down the street had been an exquisite slice of her life. She felt the same about Gus. She could join him for a drink, have spectacular sex and a warm body to sleep next to, but they avoided relationship tangles. Until now, her romantic life had mostly vacillated between marriage and nothing. She enjoyed this in between where she didn't have to tether herself to one man.

When she'd shared her new philosophy about dating with Deb, her friend had squealed with laughter. Then, she'd shared her own good news. She'd set up multiple interviews in the Bay Area and would arrive later this week and hopefully find a new job.

Lacey glanced up at the door to the apartment. Zach and Isaac wouldn't be up for hours. Sometime this afternoon, they'd check in with her and see if she needed their help around the house. She didn't, and besides, they already had a big project on their hands. They'd taken on the remodel of the cockamamie second bathroom themselves so they could bring in a roommate. With what the three of them would pay, Lacey would make far more than expected on the apartment. She saved that money. The uncertain future scared her, and she wanted to be prepared to help how she could. Perhaps money would be part of the answer.

It still terrified her to think about climate change and what that would mean for her children, for all children and all species. But whenever helplessness grasped at her, she recommitted to fighting for a better planet as long as she could.

"Mom."

Lacey turned to the gate, afraid to see a ghost she'd conjured with her thoughts. Instead, her daughter, flesh and bone, stood before her.

"Maddie!" Her heart stopped for a beat, scared to start again without this precious child. For all the joy she'd found in work and friends and family, the Maddie-sized hole in her heart often brought desolation. The thought of her bright, bossy, incredible daughter never forgiving her and letting her back into her life had resulted in more than a few late-night tears.

And here she stood on the doorstep. Tears welled in Lacey's eyes and longing filled her heart. Sean and Zach had recommended she give Maddie time. And she had refrained from calling her daughter, choosing patience over her usually demanding nature. She'd only sent a few texts, and only with the words "I will always love you." *More than the sun and the moon and the stars.* How many times had she said that to Maddie? Hundreds, maybe thousands.

Please come in. She feared if she said the words out loud, it would send her reticent daughter away. Lacey took a quiet step forward, like you would with a terrified animal, one whose previous owners had hurt it. Then another step and another.

Maddie had her own tears in her eyes. Lacey made it to the gate, opened it with barely any sound at all, then stepped through. She flung her arms around her daughter, held on with all her might. And Maddie hugged her back.

Lacey broke down in sobs. "I'm so sorry."

Maddie cried as well. She hung on to Lacey the way she had as a little girl. "No. I'm sorry, Mom."

So many thoughts raced through Lacey's mind, but one spun faster, reverberating in her mind. *It's going to be okay. It's going to be okay.* And she held on. She'd hold on forever if that's what it took.

Their tears slowed, and their breathing returned to a regular rhythm. Lacey sighed, unable to let go and melting into the folds of her daughter. Maddie felt different, more solid. Thicker.

Lacey stopped breathing and stood completely still. Maddie went rigid in her arms. Pulling back, Lacey looked into Maddie's eyes, while holding her by the elbows, just in case she tried to escape.

"Can we go inside?" Maddie asked.

"Of course." Lacey led her through the yard and up the steps. Sat her on the couch with a soft blanket over her knees. Made her herbal tea. Sat beside her and held her hand. She couldn't do enough for her daughter to make up for all that had gone before and everything left to come.

"Zach told me you got a job." Maddie cupped her tea and blew on it to cool it off. Another gesture from childhood.

"I'm volunteering, but I go in a couple of days a week to manage a project."

"I'm glad. Also, I really like your house. It's cozy here, even with the tall ceilings."

Lacey wanted to delve into more important conversations, but that would come in time, if she could just play it cool now. "I love the house, and it's great having your brother next door. I'm so sorry I didn't involve you when I bought it. I didn't want you to tell me no."

Maddie's lips pulled down at the corners of her mouth. "That might have happened. I know I've been pretty hard on you. I've been going through a lot."

Lacey patted her daughter's hand like she would have a soft cat. She wanted to calm her, let her know everything would be fine. "Is there anything I can help with?"

"I got this yesterday." She pulled something from her pocket, then handed Lacey an ultrasound image. "I'm pregnant."

Lacey wanted to hug her girl, dance, and shout to the rooftops. But that would be the wrong play. Maddie hadn't sounded happy. In fact, resigned was the best spin Lacey could put on her daughter's tone.

"And how do you feel about that?" Lacey asked.

"I've known for a while. I just couldn't admit it to myself until I saw the picture. We're having it, if that's what you want to know." The same flat-lined voice answered.

Lacey pondered the response, but in the end, her daughter's happiness mattered far more than anything else. "No. That's not what I want to know. I want to know how you feel, if you're okay."

Maddie brought her cup to her lips, blew on it once more, then took a sip, all while avoiding her mother's gaze. Finally, she responded. "I didn't want to bring a baby into this world. Injustices are growing, climate change is being ignored. I study this stuff for a living, and I can't even imagine what a terrible place the world will be by the time my child is my age."

Maddie set her mug on the coffee table and rested her hands on her belly. "I feel like I've failed my biggest task, and for some reason, I still want this baby. I kind of hate myself for that." A fresh tear rolled down her face, but with none of the sobbing of earlier.

Lacey didn't know how to address that kind of trauma. Couldn't even try. "What does Chuck think?"

Maddie humphed. "He's super happy and excited. I want to kill him."

Lacey smiled at that. Chuck would be a great dad. "You're going to be a great mom."

"That's not what I want to hear."

"Maybe not, but it's the truth. I understand your fears, and I can't stop you from worrying. Your life going forward will be full of worry, but I promise, the joy will outweigh the worry tenfold." Lacey needed to get Maddie to understand she faced yet one more task, one she could handle, one that would improve her life.

"You don't understand. My whole life has been worry—worry about the end of the world. Worry about how to stop it, and when I realized the impossibility of that, worry about how to make it a little less bad. And now, I'm going to bring new life into this disaster, but farther down the environmental tragedy. It's not fair."

"What in life is fair? It is what it is."

Maddie looked at her like she'd lost her mind. "And then you go entirely off the rails. Sell our family home, buy a retirement condo. Then that burns down. And suddenly you're all concerned about the environment, and you have no place to live. Just when I needed you most, you were completely lost."

Maddie might as well have slapped her across the face. It would have hurt less. She barely kept herself from crossing her arms and closing herself off. Instead, she stayed in the truth of those words. She had been lost, but she'd found her way to a place where she could be useful and happy. She loved the life she'd built these last months. This was her best life, one chosen exclusively by her.

"I went through a rough transition, kind of like you are now. Life is all about transitions, especially now that we've made the Earth so unpredictable. But I came out of it just fine. Maddie, I'm happier than I've ever been, even though I'm living through the last third of my life and fighting a battle I will never win. I've gained so much in terms of home and community. I didn't know life could be this good. Your part of my heart has been missing, but other than that, I'm doing great. Look around."

Lacey looked around for her. A cozy house that she loved, her son next door, her friend possibly on the way. Work she truly enjoyed and that she thought made a difference. Friends. Sex. Great food, including some she grew herself. What more could a human want?

"It's a nice house," Maddie said sullenly.

"It's more than that." Lacey took her daughter's hand. "I've built a life here that I'm proud of. I'm doing good work, just like you. You inspired me to do that. I protest with a local group, and we are determined to make change happen. I've got friends, and Zach, and hopefully you. And your family."

"Why did you have to change? Why couldn't you just be Mom? It's confusing, especially when I'm going to become a mom too. I always looked up to you."

Lacey smiled, her heart in exactly the right place. "I did my best to be a good mom to you kids, and I'm going to be a great grandmom. But what I've built now, that's what you should really be proud of. I'm finally doing all the right things."

Maddie shook her head. "I don't want to be like you anymore. I want a marriage that will work. I want stability, not to constantly change my plans."

"I love you so much," Lacey said through the hurt of her daughter's words. "My heart is full with your news and with the life I've built. I can't promise you everything will be all right. I certainly couldn't have promised myself that at the beginning of this journey. But things are better than all right. They're outstanding. I want that for you. I'm here for you."

Maddie sat quietly, looking at her hands on her belly. Perhaps aware of the life growing inside her. Lacey's heart overflowed with joy.

"I found out I was pregnant the day you announced you'd bought the house. It was much easier to be furious with you than to deal with my own fears."

"Oh, honey. I wish I'd known. I promise to be more open and honest in the future. You need to know that I'm settled here for the long haul. And I need you in my world."

"I'm sorry I've been such a pain." Maddie turned and looked at her mom. "I need you too. I'm going to need you more than ever. And you do sound better."

"Beyond better," Lacey said. "My sudden retirement tested me and made me figure out who I wanted to be. The coming crisis will test us all, but tragedy often brings out the best in people. And so much joy still exists in the world." She laid her hand on her daughter's, both of them protecting and cradling the unborn child.

"I'm so happy for you, and I want to help you find that happiness too," Lacey said. "Together we can create the best possible future. Even though the world may hurtle toward tragedy, this is still the greatest love story of my life."

And in her daughter's smile, Lacey saw all the promise the world still held. And she was overjoyed to be a part of it.

Acknowledgements

I usually save my acknowledgements for people I know who helped me through the writing of a book or the larger twists and turns of my life. This time, I'm going to do something different.

This is a book about our role in climate change, and I had some very specific teachers I've never met. Bill McKibben co-founded the nonprofit 350.org and started Third Act!. These organizations not only tell the story of climate change, they connect people to it in meaningful ways. We started it and only we can stop it. These organizations give you a way to use your power.

Andrew Boyd's book, *I Want a Better Catastrophe* opened my eyes to the range of experiences of people dealing with climate change and helped shape this novel.

Finally, Ayana Elizabeth Johnson wrote a fantastic book, *What if We Get It Right?: Visions of Climate Futures*. In an aside during a conversation with a guest, she wondered why there weren't more romance novels featuring climate change. While this novel isn't a romance, it's my effort at writing climate change into everyday life instead of focusing on an apocalypse.

My son Jack inspires me by how he attacks climate change and works for social justice on a daily basis. I love how so many people in his generation integrate these issues into their lives in a holistic way. He constantly motivates me – on the page when I write and in real life.

My husband Tom is my biggest support, a role he's embraced for over thirty years.

My most heartfelt acknowledgement goes to each person who finds this book and sticks with my quirky characters until the end. Thank you.

About the Author

Kathryn Dodson writes bold, twisty fiction where women save the day—and themselves. Kathryn grew up writing and riding horses in far west Texas. A former CEO with a PhD, a creative writing degree, and a passport full of stamps, she brings both insight and adrenaline to every story. Originally from Texas, she now lives in coastal California, where she loves fiery food, front yard happy hours, and planning her next adventure—on the page or in real life. Learn more about Kathryn and the interesting women in fascinating places she writes about—and see where her characters are headed next—at www.Kathryn Dodson.com.